THE WISHING TREE

THE WISHING TREE

CHRISTOPHER ISHERWOOD
on Mystical Religion

Edited by Robert Adjemian
Introduction by Gavin Lambert

1817

Harper & Row, Publishers, San Francisco
Cambridge, Hagerstown, New York, Philadelphia, Washington
London, Mexico City, São Paulo, Singapore, Sydney

THE WISHING TREE: *Christopher Isherwood on Mystical Religion*. Copyright © 1943, 1944, 1946, 1950, 1951, 1957, 1958, 1961, 1962, 1963, 1971, 1974, 1987 by the Vedanta Society of Southern California. For information, address the Secretary, Vedanta Society of Southern California, 1946 Vedanta Pl., Hollywood, CA 90068. Introduction © 1987 by Gavin Lambert. All rights reserved. Printed in the United States of America. No part of this book may be used or reproduced in any manner whatsoever without written permission except in the case of brief quotations embodied in critical articles and reviews. For information address Harper & Row, Publishers, Inc., 10 East 53rd Street, New York, NY 10022. Published simultaneously in Canada by Fitzhenry & Whiteside, Limited, Toronto.

FIRST EDITION
Design by Donald Hatch

Library of Congress Cataloging-in-Publication Data

Isherwood, Christopher, 1904-1986.
    The wishing tree.

    1. Vedanta.   2. Isherwood, Christopher, 1904-1986.
I. Adjemian, Robert.   II. Title.
B132.V3I76   1987   181'.48   87-45178
ISBN 0-06-250402-9 (pbk.)

87 88 89 90 91 MPC 10 9 8 7 6 5 4 3 2 1

Contents

He Belonged

Much praise, much deserved, already has been spoken of Christopher Isherwood, who died Saturday at his home in Santa Monica at the age of 81. His elegant, innovative, and unflinchingly honest prose made him one of this century's most important English-speaking writers. As such, he belonged not only to his native Britain and his adopted America, but also to the whole world of letters.

He also belonged in a special way to this city, the place in which he spent nearly half his life and where he and his art always seemed so much at home.

Isherwood was one of a group of powerful and original European artists who settled here in the 1930s as refugees. They included novelists such as Thomas Mann, Aldous Huxley, and Isherwood, dramatist Bertold Brecht, and the two giants of twentieth-century music, Arnold Schoenberg and Igor Stravinsky. Their friends and relatives remain among us, but the artists themselves are gone. They have, however, left behind a connection to and an awareness of the international avant-garde that continues to enrich and inform Los Angeles art to this day.

Things other than art also helped make Isherwood a singular man. He was a homosexual, a pacifist and a serious convert to Vedanta—an ancient Eastern creed. The concerns that arose from these personal facts were central to his work, though they never gave rise to polemics or propaganda. Rather, they produced a practical and humane spirituality that was no less real because it had transcended dogma.

Choices of the sort that Christopher Isherwood made are unfashionable, even unpopular, in today's America. Yet the life and work of the man who made them enriched us all.

Editorial in
the *Los Angeles Times*,
January 8, 1986

EDITOR'S PREFACE

In *My Guru and His Disciple* (1980), Christopher Isherwood wrote about his special and sacred relationship with Swami Prabhavananda, the founder of the Vedanta Society of Southern California.

In *The Wishing Tree* we get a glimpse into the mind of Isherwood as he tried to make sense of a crazy world through Vedanta, a philosophy that only saw perfection. Perhaps the prime question in his mind was whether he could be truthful to himself and still be religious.

At first, Isherwood was strongly antireligious. He wrote:

Religion! How that word made me wince and grit my teeth with loathing . . . I hated the Christianity I had been taught . . . God, high in heaven, ruled with grim justice over us, his sinful and brutish subjects.

Through the urging of his friends Gerald Heard and Aldous Huxley, he met Swami Prabhavananda and tried meditation.

Playing at meditation filled me with an excitement which I have seldom felt since. It was most exciting to sit on the floor in a corner of the room and feel that one was face to face with the unknown that was oneself.

But still he remembered his background. Words like *God, church,* and *sin* were unpleasant. He even told the swami that meditation was a lot of mumbo jumbo. The swami laughed and said, "And now you have fallen into the trap?"

Good or bad, Isherwood was caught. He wrote extensively about Vedanta and began translating books with Swami Prabhavananda. The antireligious attitudes within him gave way to a philosophy he could respect without compromise. Throughout much of *The Wishing Tree,* Isherwood discusses Vedanta philosophy in a way that reflects the doubts and fears of many thinking people.

"We have no use for blind believers," he wrote. With glee he discovered Swami Vivekananda:

Here at last was a man who believed in God and yet dared to condemn the indecent groveling of the sin-obsessed Puritans I had so much despised in my youth. I loved him at once, for his bracing self-reliance, his humor, and his courage. He appealed to me as the perfect anti-Puritan hero: the enemy of Sunday religion, the destroyer of Sunday gloom, the shocker of prudes, the breaker of traditions, the outrager of conventions, the comedian who taught the deepest truths in idiotic jokes and frightful puns. That humor had its place in religion, that it could actually be a mode of self-expression, was a revelation to me.

Devout Christians should not be offended by this vehemence. Isherwood did not care to criticize how other people approached God. He had great respect for those with genuine and sincere beliefs, as long as they didn't feel urged by God to convert him.

From another standpoint, the fact remains that many good people are offended by Western religion. The spirit of Christopher Isherwood's writings is dedicated to those who feel that they could never be religious, to those branded sinners by the church, for they are his own kin.

———————

This collection of articles was written by Christopher Isherwood for the Vedanta Society of Southern California from 1943 to 1975. Most of these pieces appeared in the magazine *Vedanta and the West;* a few were written as prefaces to books published by Vedanta Press or were given as talks and later prepared for publication. Excluding the articles that were actually excerpts from complete books, we have included here almost all of his writings from that period.

These writings are essentially unknown to the general public, yet they represent some of Isherwood's best work as an author. It is difficult to explain the concepts of the East to a westerner, and even more so to do it with beauty. That Christopher Isherwood has done this so well will be of interest to both the student of his writings and the spiritual seeker.

—Robert Adjemian

INTRODUCTION:
CERTAIN SIGNALS

Meditate on the Real Self. The Self in you is the Self in all beings. Christopher Isherwood received this instruction from Swami Prabhavananda soon after they met in the summer of 1939. In fact, most of Isherwood's writing up to this point had been a form of meditation on his Real Self, but instead of guiding him toward the "infinite Bliss" that Prabhavananda considered to be its goal, it had left him close to despair. Soon after arriving in New York in January 1939, he wrote to a friend; "I am in the most Goddamawful mess." For not only was he creatively dry, but he had lost his political faith and could find nothing to put in its place except a negative pacifism, a blank, scared refusal "to take any part in the war effort, if war came."

Hoping to find out a way out of the mess, Isherwood went on to Los Angeles, where Gerald Heard and Aldous Huxley had settled two years earlier. Both of them, he knew, were active pacifists—and although he'd heard they were also involved with Hinduism or Vedanta, he planned to sidestep "all this Oriental stuff" and concentrate on the main issue. But after a few conversations with Heard, he began to suspect "all this Oriental stuff" might be the main issue after all; and after a few conversations with Prabhavananda, he was certain of it. The personal impact of the man was so overwhelming that Isherwood found it impossible to disbelieve in the swami's belief and arrived at perhaps the most unexpected turning point of his life.

Long before terms like *faction* and *nonfiction novel* became fashionable, autobiography and fiction overlapped in Isherwood's work. His first directly autobiographical book, *Lions and Shadows,* appeared in 1938, and the preface advised us to "read it like a novel," because it used a novelist's license in recreating characters and incidents from his life in the twenties. The fiction of the same period, including *Goodbye to Berlin* (1939), had its origins in fact—the extensive diaries that Isherwood began in 1929; and these diaries, which he kept until 1982, also supply the basic material for all his later work. But the earlier Isherwood, unlike the later one, was deeply alienated from himself and the world. In *Lions and Shadows,* the mirror reflects an image that he describes as "familiar, tiresome, despicable," and he feels he can escape from it only by escaping from England, the motherland symbolized by his own mother, whom he believes wants Isherwood to reflect *her* own image—comfortable, respectable, upper-class puritanism.

Initially, leaving England to live in Berlin was an escape to sexual freedom, but Isherwood discovered other freedoms there. Exile in itself was liberating; by not being "at home" one gained a broader sense of perspective on the world as a whole. With the Nazis beginning to emerge from the wings, he knew he was living, like Berlin itself, on borrowed time. After the static complacency of England, this was liberating as well. It sharpened his responses, encouraged detachment, and he came to appreciate the lasting value of a sense of impermanence.

But by 1933 the Nazis had moved to center stage, and Isherwood left a city that lay, as he wrote in *Goodbye to Berlin,* "under an epidemic of discreet, infectious fear. I could feel it, like influenza, in my bones . . ." During the rest of his time in Europe, the fear became less discreet and more naked. In *Journey to a War* (1939), written after a visit to China with Auden, he described an air raid at night, comparing distant Japanese planes in the sky to "the bacilli of a fatal disease" and transforming the scene into a deadly H. G. Wells fantasy. By the time Isherwood arrived in the United States, the fatal bacilli had begun to spread, and the epidemic of World War II was expected to break out at any moment. Under this enormous threat, nothing could stand up. His sense of detachment crumbled, for how to detach oneself from an overwhelming fear of war? During the thirties he had shared the hopeful left-wing beliefs of his friends, but they seemed meaningless now. Unlike Auden, who had his own eccentric brand of Christianity to fall back on, Isherwood was hostile to the whole idea of religion. Without convictions or bearings of any kind, he suddenly found himself—until he met Prabhavananda—with nowhere to go.

The "occasional" articles that Isherwood wrote about Vedanta from 1943 onward interpret its philosophy for the West with his usual directness and clarity—and, like his work as a whole, they are also autobiographical. His contact with Prabhavananda, of course, was the original impulse behind them; and like the diaries, but in capsule form, they supply the basic material for Isherwood as a writer. You can read them today not only for themselves, but for the shock of recognition. They summarize ideas and experiences that the novelist and self-chronicler develops in all his later fiction and nonfiction.

Religion, he wrote in "What Vedanta Means to Me," "is not taught by one intelligence to another but caught through the influence of one personality upon another. . . . As far as I am concerned, the guru-disciple relationship is at the center of everything that religion means to me." But at the time of writing the article (1951), Isherwood didn't "even begin to understand" the process involved and didn't try to describe it. He only knew that it was a reality he never doubted. More than thirty years passed before he understood it fully, and it took more than time to provide a perspective. Prabhavananda had died before Isherwood began writing *My Guru and His Disciple* (1980), that extraordinary spiritual love story in which the author casts himself as a prodigal son and Prabhavananda as the father with whom—in spite of occasional rebellions—he feels an unbreakable tie.

Their relationship is portrayed with the skill of a novelist at the height of his powers who happens to be writing nonfiction, and the swami emerges as perhaps the most mysteriously convincing saint in literature. Many years earlier, in "Who Is Ramakrishna?" (1957), Isherwood had commented on the great teacher's "extraordinary mixture of simplicity, fun, and strangeness"; and in another article, "The Problem of the Religious Novel" (1946), on the stereotyped saint, remote and humorless, "set apart from this bad world" and "the dreariest of bores." The Prabhavananda of *My Guru and His Disciple* is a joyful antistereotype, chain-smoking, belching, energetic, worldly-wise as well as unworldly, in manner more like a disciple than a teacher, gentle and loving, and occasionally sentimental—he adored the movie of *Song of Bernadette*—in spite of his past as a student revolutionary who knew how to handle a gun.

In "What Vedanta Means to Me" and "What Is Vedanta?" (1944), Isherwood explains the decisive (for him) appeal of a philosophy that rejects Christian dualism, refusing to set spirit against flesh, vice against virtue, this world against the next, and declining the idea of original sin in favor of something far more positive. For it dwells instead "on the greatness of man's eternal nature," and on life as "an active search for awareness"—of a Reality that lies in the secret union, the interrelatedness of every creature and object in this world, beneath the changing outward appearance of things.

To discover this Reality is also to discover one's real nature; this is what happens to the protagonist of Isherwood's last-but-one and most powerful novel, *A Single Man* (1964). A middle-aged Los Angeles professor, George, is truly single—sad and lost after the death of his lover in the recent past, scared of a lonely, cranky, senior citizen future. But by the end of a day and a night, he was moved outside himself, beyond the pain of separateness, through a chance encounter with a student. The encounter itself will probably not lead to anything, but George no longer feels trapped in a closed, solitary limbo. He is on the human market now, open to offers, and with something to offer. The season of the single man is over.

There's an echo of the same idea in another novel, *Down There on a Visit* (1962), and in two autobiographical books, *Kathleen and Frank* (1971), and *Christopher and His Kind* (1976). In all of them, through the device of a spiritual flashback, Isherwood returns to his past; and as the older, Vedantist writer looks back on the younger one, he perceives what he failed to perceive in himself and others at the time. But behind all of them seems to lie another idea, first noted in a lecture, "On Girish Ghosh" (ca. 1957). One of Ramakrishna's most profound insights, Isherwood commented then, was that "all our so-called vices are in fact frustrated attempts to find the truth, or to find peace, or to find release from something." *Down There on a Visit* consists of four episodes in which the younger Isherwood spent a season in somebody else's hell during the thirties and early forties, but it's only much later that he *relates* them—in both meanings of the word. Looking back, he can see that he was searching for release from a hell of his own and was drawn to others in the same situation, but too unaware to make the connection.

In *Kathleen and Frank,* Isherwood explores his family history. Reading his mother's diaries after her death, he revises his opinion of her as a destructive force and sees that the years of mutual antagonism were years of painful evolution for both of them. In retrospect, they seem to have been much closer to each other than they realized and too proud or obstinate to send out peace signals. And missed connections recur in *Christopher and His Kind*. Recalling his life in Berlin, when the anti-son was in sexual and political revolt against Kathleen's world, the older writer recognizes the younger one at a vital stage in his education. But when he remembers the actual lives he fictionalized in the collected *Berlin Stories* (1946), he finds the earlier Isherwood lacking in a wider awareness—failing again to look beyond himself, to respond to the human desperation in so-called vice, to interpret and exchange signals.

"One day, the two human mysteries known to this world as Bernhardt and Vivekananda met, exchanged certain signals which we do not understand, and parted, we do not know why. All we do know is that their meeting, like every other event in this universe, did not take place by accident."

This is Isherwood's comment on a meeting that took place, sometime in 1900, in the dressing room of the famous actress. "Vivekananda and Sarah Bernhardt" (1943) is the most "novelistic" of his essays on Vedanta, for Bernhardt's biographers never recorded the meeting. It survives as history only in a few casual yet vivid references in letters written by the swami to an Indian friend. They mention that Bernhardt expressed her "special regard for India," and that she longed to go there but didn't have the money. Vivekananda affectionately doubts this—she *would* have the money, he writes, if she didn't spend so lavishly. Apart from a few more details of Bernhardt's fascination with India that the swami relays to his friend, nothing more is known. Yet it's enough for the novelist, and the Vedantist, to reach further and arrive at the heart of the matter.

Certain signals—they are not verbal and have to be read between the lines, or "below the threshold of everyday awareness," because their medium is "more direct, more subtle and more penetrating" than talk. And they make their first appearance in Isherwood's first novel written in America, while he was living at the Vedanta Center. *Prater Violet* (1945) takes place during the thirties, when Isherwood was in London for a few months writing a screenplay for the exiled Viennese director, Bergmann. "There are meetings which are like recognitions," wrote Isherwood—and when the young writer is introduced to the middle-aged Jew he sees "the face of a political situation, an epoch." But by the end of their collaboration, he also saw his own image in Bergmann's, for two exiles have found a temporary home in each other. As described in the novel, they are walking together at night, each lost in his own thoughts, not speaking, and Isherwood realizes that "beneath outer consciousness, two other beings, anonymous, impersonal, without labels, have met and recognized each other and clasped hands. . . . " The moment looks ahead to many similar ones— to George in *A Single Man* (1964), after he goes swimming with the student in the Pacific at night and feels that "*some kind of a signal*" has been exchanged between two people physically naked and stripped of their outer selves, communicating without words; to the two deeply estranged brothers in the last novel, *A Meeting by the River* (1967), who reconcile at last by kissing each other, then breaking into uncontrollable laughter; and even to an exchange of signals with the dead, the suicide and the drug addict in *Down There on a Visit,* Kathleen, the "real" Sally Bowles and others from the *Berlin Stories,* remembered and contacted on a deeper level many years later.

And near the end of his life, Isherwood received a certain signal from himself. *October* (1980), his last published work, is a collaboration with his "ideal companion," Don Bachardy; its text a journal written especially for the book, its illustrations drawings made by Bachardy during the same month. In the first day's entry Isherwood writes that he often wakes up "in a state of inexplicable happiness." This is not a state that appeals to literary critics. They have always preferred the religious writers, from Dostoevsky to Graham Greene, who tell us in effect, "I suffer, therefore I am." The Vedanta approach, with its declared aim of enlightenment as joy, has never been seriously fashionable or fashionably serious, and the idea persists that to offer a way out of suffering is somehow a compromise. Yet Isherwood's life and work refute it, and the articles in this book provide a glimpse behind the scenes of disciplines not easily won or maintained, of a gradual journey toward a state of mysterious, dynamic peace—beautifully described in this verse from *The*

Bhagavad-Gita, which he translated in collaboration with Swami Prabhavananda:

> Worn-out garments
> Are shed by the body:
> Worn-out bodies
> Are shed by the dweller
> Within the body.
> New bodies are donned
> By the dweller, like garments . . .

—Gavin Lambert

PART I

HOW I CAME TO VEDANTA

Left to right: Swami Prabhavananda, Aldous Huxley, and Christopher Isherwood at the Vedanta Society in Hollywood in the 1940s. (Photograph courtesy of the Vedanta Society of Southern California.)

How I Came to Vedanta

Toward the end of January 1939, I arrived with W. H. Auden in New York by boat from England.

Why had I come to America? I suppose because I couldn't stop traveling; I had become constitutionally restless. The mechanism had been set going during the six years since Hitler's seizure of power and my consequent departure from Germany, which I had almost begun to regard as home; six years of wandering around Western Europe from Sweden to Spain, ending up with a trip to China with Auden in 1938. And now America was the obvious next move. We had had a brief, melodramatic glimpse of it the previous summer, on our way home from the Far East. We had shot up and down skyscrapers, in and out of parties and bars; we had watched a fight in a Bowery dive, heard Maxine Sullivan sing in Harlem, been at Coney Island on July the Fourth. I had gone back to England raving about Manhattan, convinced, like most tourists, that New York is the United States.

However, the Christopher who now returned to New York was no longer quite the same Christopher who had left it five months before. For one thing, I had just realized—while we were crossing the Atlantic—that I was a pacifist.

Maybe it would be more exact to say: I realized that I had always been a pacifist. At any rate, in the negative sense. How could I have ever imagined that I was anything else? My earliest remembered feelings of rebellion were against the British Army, in which my father was a regular officer, and against the staff of my first boarding school, who tried, with the best intentions, to make me believe in a glamorized view of the 1914–18 war and of my father's death in it. My father had taught me, by his life and death, to hate the profession of soldiering. I remember his telling me, before he left for France, that an officer's sword is useless except for toasting bread, and that he never fired his revolver because he couldn't hit anything with it and hated the bang. He was killed while leading an attack, carrying only a swagger stick with which he was signaling directions to his men. I adored my father's memory, dwelling always on his civilian virtues: his gentleness, his humor, his musical and artistic talent. Growing up into the postwar world, I learnt to loathe the old men who had made the war. Flags, uniforms, and war memorials made me tremble with rage because they filled me with terror. I was horribly scared by the idea of war and therefore subconsciously attracted to it.

However, in 1936, a war broke out which seemed, at first, to present a clear-cut issue between right and wrong: the Civil War in Spain. I joined my friends—and the vast majority of English writers—in supporting the Republican government. We believed that the government, being absolutely in the right, was entitled to use any means available to overcome its enemies. So my pacifism was temporarily forgotten. And, like my friends, I greeted the entry of Soviet Russia into the Popular Front as an ally, even though most of us had been shocked by the injustice shown in the Moscow treason trials of the early thirties.

Auden had already visited Spain, early in the war. Toward the end of 1937, I arranged to go with him to Madrid as part of a delegation of English writers and artists sympathetic to the government cause. But this visit was repeatedly postponed by the Spanish authorities, and in the meantime Auden and I had been offered a contract by our publishers to write a book about any country in the Far East. So we decided to leave in January 1938 for China. China had lately been invaded by the Japanese and was in a situation somewhat similar to that of Spain; a (more or less) democratic government attacked by unprovoked aggressors.

I have already indicated one of my motives for wanting to get into a ringside seat at a war: the fascination of one's own fear, a motive many people must have for going big game hunting. Also, of course, there was ordinary healthy excitement and wanderlust. Also, there was genuine concern for the victims of aggression and a desire to make their wrongs known to the rest of the world—yes, there was a little, at least, of that too.

As a mater of fact, our visit to wartime China did me a great deal of good. First, it reduced my neurotic fear of war in the abstract. True, our journey through the combat zone wasn't really very dangerous. I think there were only three or four occasions on which we were at all likely to have been killed by bombs or bullets. But a very little danger will go a long way, psychologically. Several times I was afraid, but only healthily afraid. I now no longer dreaded some unknown horror or feared that I should behave much worse than other people in the same circumstances.

Secondly, the visit to China brought me back from a world of political principles to a world of human values which I had temporarily lost. In China I saw boys in their early teens who had been conscripted to serve in the front-line trenches. I saw the corpses of old men and women killed in an air raid. I smelled the rotting bodies of wounded soldiers dying of gas gangrene. War starts with principles but it ends with people— people who have usually little or no interest in the principles. This was an obvious fact which I had been overlooking; and nothing hits you harder than the obvious, when you suddenly become aware of it. I found I didn't dare to say that these people ought to die in defense of any principles whatsoever, no matter how noble or right. In fact, balanced against this suffering and death, all such questions of right and wrong seemed academic and irrelevant. My own acceptance of armed force as a means of political action had been due simply to a lack of feeling and imagination. *That* I knew was true—at least as far as I myself was concerned. I couldn't speak for others. If they honestly believed in the rightness of fighting, *and* were prepared to prove their honesty by risking their own lives, then I would honor them and try to imitate their courage in following my own path. But for the future I myself must be an avowed pacifist.

(I must pause here to make one point as clear as I can. In this statement, I am not trying to present a general case in favor of pacifism. I am describing my own feelings as they related to a series of situations; and I am only doing this in order to explain how they brought me into touch with the ideas of Vedanta. Therefore, it is useless for the reader to ask me indignantly, "Can you pretend that you would still be a pacifist if you belonged to a racial minority threatened with extermination?" I can't tell him. I haven't been in that situation. So I don't know.)

Such was my decision, as it finally became clear to me. But for a while nothing was clear. The autumn of 1938 was a period of confusion for all of us. There was the climax and anticlimax of Munich. There was the tragedy of the crumbling of the Spanish government, destroyed from within quite as much as from without; allies accusing each other of treason and the clear-seeming lines of political integrity becoming more and more distorted. There was the emerging possibility of almost indefinite Nazi expansion without general war.

Clear thinking was impossible during the Munich crisis. It was impossible as long as I was lecturing to audiences on our Chinese journey, and thereby identifying myself with China's armed resistance to the Japanese invasion. But the voyage to New York provided a break for thought in the midst of all this compulsive activity. I had time to ask myself where I stood.

Thus I accepted the fact that I was a pacifist. If war came, I would refuse to fight. That was all I had left to go on with: a negation. For, as I now began to realize, my whole political position, left-wing antifascist, had been based on the acceptance of armed force. All the slogans I had been repeating and living by were essentially militaristic. Very well; throw them out. But what remained? I told myself that I should have to put my emotions back from a political on to a personal basis. I would be an individual again, with my own values, my own kind of integrity. This sounded challenging and exciting. But it raised a disconcerting question: what were the values to be?

In the mid-1920s, when I was a very young man, I had taken as my ideal the figure of The Artist, as it is presented by the romantic writers of the nineteenth century. The Artist stands alone; this is his tragedy and his glory. He is isolated from the common crowd by the superior fineness of his perceptions. His work is therefore generally misunderstood and condemned. He is scorned, persecuted, let starve, sometimes even imprisoned or put to death. All this he suffers, because he refuses to disguise the truth as he sees it. Baudelaire, in his famous poem, compares The Poet to an albatross whose giant wings prevent him from walking on the ground which symbolizes dull common everyday life. He is presented as a dedicated and holy figure—a martyr and in his own way a saint.

Later, at the beginning of the 1930s, I passed, like most of my friends, into a socially conscious political phase. What were important, we now declared, were the needs and wrongs of the common man. The function of art was to proclaim them. We wanted to expose abuses and denounce tyrants and exploiters. We wanted to point the way to a happier era of peace and plenty, equality and civil justice. We were utopian socialists. If our critics called us propagandists, we agreed with them proudly. "All art is propaganda," we replied. "Intentionally or unintentionally, it is bound to express some kind of philosophy, either reactionary or progressive. The merit we claim for *our* propaganda is that it is both progressive and intentional."

Since we were concerned with the common man and the welfare of the exploited many, we were unavoidably critical and hostile in our attitude toward the few. Everything uncommon and private had become suspect by us. We now sneered at the romantic ideal of The Artist. His private sensibilities and his alienation from the masses no longer impressed us; we had decided that his predicament was merely due to neurosis.

Such had been my philosophy during the 1930s. Now I was discarding it in favor of some kind of individualism, at present ill defined. It seemed to me that I knew only what I *didn't* want, what I *couldn't* accept.

I couldn't accept, any longer, this attitude of self-abasement before the concepts of the Masses and the Common Man; it now seemed to me masochistic and insincere. It seemed to me that I had been confusing a valid concern for the victims of injustice with an invalid and almost idolatrous cult of the majority *as* a majority. As a matter of fact, I didn't like or respect majorities or believe that they must necessarily be in the right; I only feared them and therefore wished to propitiate them. As for the Common Man (if such a being exists) I didn't honestly think that he must always be possessed of a superior wisdom about life. I was still ready to admit that there might be things he could teach me, but I now cast false humility aside and claimed that there were things I could teach *him*. Why should either of us humble himself before the other?

But though I was proposing to live a less political and more personal life, I couldn't, ever again, be an individualist in the old sense. I had discovered that I had been too much involved in politics, or involved in the wrong way; but I knew that I must never dare to ignore what was going on in the world around me. And whenever I met social injustice on the personal level, I must try to take up its challenge.

Moreover, I couldn't any longer accept The Artist as my ideal—for, as I now realized, I no longer believed in Art as an absolute aim and justification of a human life. Certainly I still intended to write books; but writing, in itself, wasn't enough for me. It might occupy most of my time, but it couldn't be my means of spiritual support, my religion.

Religion! How the word still made me wince and grit my teeth with loathing! I had declared myself an atheist at the age of twenty and now, at nearly thirty-five, I hadn't changed my opinion. I had no expectation that I should ever do so. Religion, I was prepared to tell all and sundry, was evil, superstitious, reactionary nonsense, and those who propagated it were enemies of progress and of mankind.

But what did I mean by *religion?*

By *religion* I meant the Christian religion as I had encountered it through the Church of England, into which I had been baptized as a baby and confirmed as a teenage boy. I regarded the Hindus, Buddhists, and Muslims as picturesque heathens merely. I didn't think of them as being "religious" at all.

I hated Christianity—the kind of Christianity I had been taught—because it was dualistic. God, high in heaven, ruled with grim justice over us, his sinful and brutish subjects, here below. He was good. We were bad. We were so bad that we crucified Jesus his son, whom he had sent down to live amongst us. For this crime, committed nearly two thousand years ago, each new generation had to beg forgiveness. If we begged hard enough and were sincerely sorry, we might be sent to purgatory and even eventually let into heaven, instead of being thrown into hell where we by rights belonged.

Who—I furiously exclaimed—wouldn't rebel against the concept of such a God? Who wouldn't abhor his tyranny? Who wouldn't denounce the cruel unfairness of this test he had set us: one short human life in which to earn salvation or damnation? Who wouldn't detest his Son, who had come to us—like a vice squad officer bent on entrapment—wearing a hypocritical mask of meekness in order to tempt us to murder him? Such were the questions I asked; and my answer was that only slaves could accept such a religion. In the Christian hell one could expect to meet every honest and courageous man or woman who had ever lived. If hell existed, then I for one would be proud to be damned.

But hell, I added, *didn't* exist. And neither did God, with his laws and his punishments. The whole thing was, only too obviously, a fiction invented by schoolmasters and policemen; a projection of their own morbid guilt complexes and life hatred.

When I looked at the Christians around me, I chose to see them as a collection of dreary canting hypocrites, missionaries of ignorance and reaction, who opposed all social reform lest it should endanger the status and privileges of their Church, and all personal freedom lest the individual should discover for himself that the "don'ts" they preached were unnecessary. I loathed their gravity, their humility, their lack of humor, their special tone when speaking of their God. I believed, or pretended to believe, that every Christian was secretly longing to indulge in forbidden pleasures, and that he was only prevented from doing so by his cowardice, ugliness, or impotence. I delighted in stories which told of clergymen being seduced, and monks and nuns carrying on clandestine love affairs. My malice against them knew no bounds. At the same time, I proudly declared that I myself needed no religion to keep me moral, according to my own standards. I tried to behave more or less decently because I freely chose to follow the advice of my own conscience; *I* didn't need the Ten Commandments to nudge me, or the fear of an absurd medieval nightmare called hell.

I have no doubt that these exaggerated reactions were, to some extent, produced by certain experiences in my boyhood which had given me a dread of authority. Certainly, my violence on this subject approached hysteria. But this isn't important, as far as my present narrative is concerned. For my prejudices, neurotic though they may have been, had also a relation to the reasonable criticisms which can be made of conventional Christianity. They were by no means utterly unjustified. And they had to be reasonably dealt with before I could get out of my philosophical dead end and find myself another road.

This second visit of mine to New York was a disaster, almost from the start. The conquering confident mood in which I had approached America quickly disappeared. It had been based on the illusions of a tourist, and now I was a tourist no longer. I wanted to make my own niche in American life and settle down and get to work. But I found that I couldn't write a line. I was paralyzed by apprehension. The high cost of our living scared me. So did the European news, which got steadily worse; until war seemed almost inevitable. The hospitality of friends and strangers couldn't reassure me, for I felt that I was accepting it under false pretenses. The Christopher Isherwood they wanted to see was no longer myself—for he represented those very attitudes and beliefs I had just abandoned. For the same reason, I was most unwilling to teach or give lectures: I could no longer tell an audience the things they expected to hear from me—and I certainly couldn't appear before them with a new "message." There was no conceivable statement I could venture to make at this point in my life, except "I don't know."

As the weeks went by, my sense of insecurity became more and more acute. I began to realize that, whatever else I did, I must get away from New York. In New York, I was, to a minor degree, a public figure—and one which had, in reality, ceased to exist. Now I desperately needed anonymity, time to think, and someone to help me do my thinking. Where should I go? Who would help me?

I had first met Gerald Heard in London in 1930. At that time, his chief interests were prehistory, the evolution of man, the advances of modern science on its various fronts, and the investigation of psychic phenomena. He had written a number of books, but his friends agreed that his greatest brilliance was shown in his lectures, radio talks, and conversation. He had, and has, a genius for communicating to others the fervor of his own interest in any subject he discusses.

In 1937, Gerald Heard, Aldous and Maria Huxley, and a

close friend of mine named Christopher Wood had all left England and settled in California, in the Los Angeles area. Rumors had reached us that Gerald was now devoting himself to the study of yoga. My friends and I had laughed over this; we pictured him levitating with Huxley in turbans and floating out over the desert at a great altitude. But the rumor, even if true didn't at all shake my faith in Gerald's basic integrity. It seemed right for him to be investigating any kind of esoteric lore, the more disreputable the better. For he had the curiosity of the truly intelligent, combined with a sane skepticism which isn't afraid to find mud around the well of truth. The fact that some mediums are fakes had never driven him into the ranks of those intellectual cowards who—largely because of their terror of being laughed at—denounce psychical research as mere self-deception. If Gerald was temporarily interested in these yogis, or yogas, or swamis, or whatever they were called—then good luck to him, I said. I knew that his findings would at any rate make an excellent story, because Gerald is one of the greatest storytellers alive.

It was not as a yoga-adept, however that I now appealed to him, but as a pacifist. Both he and Aldous Huxley had already declared their pacifism in various books and articles. We exchanged letters. Gerald wrote that "every pacifist should acquire medical knowledge . . . creative accuracy must be opposed to disorder and destruction. . . . We must create a doctorate of psychologically sound, well-equipped healers." This sounded authoritative and encouraging, even if somewhat vague. I certainly knew that I needed discipline of some kind in my own life—and the idea of being a healer, in whatever sense, appealed to me, who had once seriously considered becoming a doctor.

And thus I decided to leave for California. I wanted to have some long talks with Gerald and find out exactly what he meant, and what he had discovered. I wanted to hear from Christopher Wood—an Englishman of my own age, with whom I could closely identify myself—how he had managed to settle down and adjust to American life. I wanted to meet Aldous and Maria

Huxley. And then there was my ever itching wanderlust. The "real" America of my daydreams had always been the Far West. Wishing to see the country through the eyes of one of its natives, I persuaded a young footloose artist to come with me. We set off early in May, with very little money, on a Greyhound bus.

In contrast with New York, Hollywood (where we first settled) seemed a sanctuary—simply because of the presence of my friends. Chris Wood reassured me just as I had hoped he would, by helping me over the difficult period of getting accustomed to this familiar-foreign land. He also took away most of my material worries by lending me enough money to live on until I eventually got work as a movie writer. And as for Gerald, he did indeed answer many of my questions—and, at the same time, caused me to ask twice as many new ones.

I have difficulty at this point in my narrative because I must now try to tell in a logical, tidy way what it was that Gerald had to say to me. I must begin at the beginning. But such dialogues between human beings—carried on throughout a series of meetings and over a period of months—never do begin at the beginning or end at the end. They jump from topic to topic, turn around upon themselves, are inconsequent and repetitious. Therefore I must present what follows in a falsely stylized and simplified manner.

This is *not* the story of a conversion through intellectual conviction. Is anyone ever convinced of anything by pure reason alone? Well, I suppose it is possible that pure reason could lead you to choose one make of electric toaster out of several. But that is, surely, never the way in which the decisive convictions of our lives are arrived at. The right teacher must appear at exactly the right moment in the right place; and his pupil must be in the right mood to accept what he teaches. Then—and only then—can argument and reason exert their full power. Surely we can all agree on that? And yet so many autobiographers distort their narratives by presenting themselves as creatures who make all decisions rationally and change their opinions just because they have been intellectually convinced that they should do so! I hope to avoid that error here.

I must start, then, by making it clear that I put Gerald— not once but over and over again during the months that followed—to the test of my intuition—not an infallible test, to be sure, but, in the long run, the best that any of us can settle for, short of mathematical certainty. Watching him carefully— making all due allowance for his love of arresting phrases and ingenious analogies, and for the powerfully persuasive beauty of his voice—I had to say to myself: No, he isn't lying, either to me or to himself. And he isn't crazy. I know this man. He speaks the same language I do. He accepts the same values. If this is true for him, then I'm forced to admit that it must be true for me, too.

Although I had just traveled three thousand miles to see Gerald, this was still a disturbing thought: that, if Gerald *was* sane, I couldn't afford to ignore his ideas. I should have to study them, perhaps act on them. Gerald, I could see, was expecting that I should. He had the air of having waited for my arrival as one waits for a valuable recruit—an assistant, almost. Very few people, he flatteringly hinted, ever came to "this thing" (his favorite synonym for the matter of his investigations). Only one man in ten thousand would take an interest at all. And of those ten thousand, only one would do anything about it. "It's only when the sheer *beastliness* of the world begins to hurt you—like crushing your finger in a door—it's only then that you'll be ready to take this step."

What step?

I can't exactly remember, after all these years, just what it was that I had expected Gerald to be doing—what I had supposed "yoga" to be all about. Some kind of ritualistic practices, no doubt, partaking of black magic, along with a study of the cabala (whatever that was), crystal gazing, tarot pack reading, and maybe some breathing exercises which would enable one, when sufficiently adept, to be buried alive. Probably,

I hadn't bothered to picture anything clearly. I had merely sneered.

This "yoga" in which Gerald was so passionately interested had, I now learned, nothing whatsoever to do with fortune-telling, scrying, or casting spells. A small branch of it, called hatha yoga, did, it was true, deal in breathing exercises—but Gerald didn't practice these. The swami was against them. He said they were dangerous if carried to excess and might lead to hallucinations.

("Who is 'the swami'?" I asked. "Swami Prabhavananda," Gerald answered, "I want you to meet him soon.")

Gerald explained that *yoga* is a Sanskrit word—the ancestor of our English word *yoke*—and that it means, basically, "union." Yoga is a method—any one of many methods—by which the individual can achieve union with God.

(Probably, Gerald never actually used the word *God* during this first stage of my indoctrination. He was wise enough to avoid it—knowing only too well from his own experience how repulsive it must be to a refugee from Christian dualism like myself. Besides, "God" in the Yoga sense is a quite different concept from that of "God" in the Christian sense. But more of that, later.)

Yoga philosophy teaches that we have two selves—an apparent, outer self and an invisible, inner self. The apparent self claims to be an individual and as such, other than all other individuals. It calls itself by a name, seeks its own advantage, is anxious, cheerful, afraid, bold, lustful, enraged, hungry, thirsty, sleepy, cold, hot, healthy, sick, young, or old, as the ever altering case may be. The real self is unchanging and immortal; it has no individuality, for it is equally within every human being, living creature, vegetable, mineral, and inanimate object. Or, to put it in another way, there is a part of myself which, being infinite, has access to the infinite—as the sea water in a bay has access to the sea because it *is* the sea.

Therefore, yoga is the process of exploring your own nature;

of finding out what it really is. It is the process of becoming aware of your real situation. The day-to-day space-time "reality" (as it is reported to us by our senses in the daily newspapers) is, in fact, no reality at all, but a deadly and cunning illusion. The practice of yoga meditation consists in excluding, as far as possible, our consciousness of the illusory world, the surface "reality," and turning the mind inward in search of its real nature. Our real nature is to be one with life, with consciousness, with everything else in the universe. The fact of oneness is the real situation. Supposed individuality, separateness, and division are merely illusion and ignorance. Awareness is increased through love (or, as Gerald preferred to call it, "interest-affection") and weakened by hatred; since love strengthens the sense of oneness and hatred the sense of separateness. Hence all positive feeling and action toward other people is in one's deepest interests, and all negative feeling and action finally harm oneself.

It should be obvious, from the above, why Gerald had to be a pacifist; any support of military force, on his part—however partial or carefully qualified—would have been a denial of his basic beliefs. Nevertheless, Gerald's pacifism might well have been attacked by those pacifists who believe in political action—demonstrations, hunger strikes, and the tactics of nonviolence. Such people no doubt described him as a quietist, a too passive observer of the catastrophe toward which the world was heading. Throughout the 1939–45 war, Gerald was in fact always ready to offer sympathy and practical advice to those young conscientious objectors who had gotten into difficulties with the authorities; but he himself was by nature philosophically detached. He had little belief in the efficacy of political action. He was constantly reminding us that free will does not operate—as we wishfully imagine it does—in the sphere of present events; averting this danger, gaining that advantage. No—at any given moment of action, we are tied hand and foot, because our present problems are created by our past deeds and thoughts.

We have to do whatever we have already made it inevitable that we shall do. In the sphere of events, we can affect the working out of the future; we can do nothing to touch the present moment. Free will, applied to the present moment, consists simply in this: no matter what is happening to us, we can, at any moment, turn away from or toward our real nature. We can deny its existence or affirm it. We can forget its presence or remember it. We can act and think in a way that will bring us closer to it or alienate us from it.

And now—leaving theory and getting down to practice— how in fact are we to turn toward and affirm the existence of our real nature? In two ways, Gerald said. Firstly, by living in such a manner as to remove the obstacles to self-knowledge. Secondly, by the regular practice of meditation.

The obstacles to self-knowledge came under three heads— Gerald had a tidy mind and was apt to speak of the universal truths in terms of a filing system—addictions, possessions, and pretensions. Addictions (which included also aversions: anything from chain-smoking to a horror of cats) were, according to him, the least harmful of the three. Pretensions were the worst, because, when you are free of all sensual attachments and all your superfluous belongings, when you have forgiven all your enemies and said good-bye to all your lovers, when you have resigned from all your positions of honor and ceased to use your titles of nobility—then, and only then, are you liable to fall victim to the spiritual arrogance which can become the worst obstacle of all.

Much of this "intentional living" (another of Gerald's phrases) must obviously be negative in character, since it is concerned with self-discipline. The positive side of one's effort to gain self-knowledge was to be found in the practice of meditation. At this time, Gerald himself was meditating six hours a day; two in the morning, two at noon, two at night. He made light of this truly intimidating schedule, saying that it was really a minimum, as far as he was concerned. If he didn't constantly remind himself of "this thing" during at least six of his waking hours, he feared that he would lose touch with it altogether. This left the rest of us free to draw the obvious conclusion.

What did Gerald actually do when he meditated? What did he think about? Gerald seemed unwilling to answer these questions very specifically. It was a private matter, I gathered. There were no general rules. Each individual would arrive at his own methods, in accordance with his own needs and temperament. Gerald himself had his instructions from Swami Prabhavananda, who would doubtless instruct me also if I asked him to do so. In the meanwhile, until I had made up my mind to go seriously into pursuit of "this thing," Gerald said it would do me no harm to practice short "sits." I wasn't to set myself any program of meditation. I wasn't to *try* to meditate at all. I was merely to sit quiet, for ten or fifteen minutes twice a day, morning and evening. I was to remind myself of "this thing," what it was and why I wanted it.

This I said I would do—and I did do it, now and then. This kind of playing at meditation filled me with an excitement which I have seldom felt since. It was most exciting to sit on the floor in a corner of the room, in the darkness of early morning or evening, and feel that one was face to face with the unknown that was oneself. This was a sort of flirtation with the unconscious—made exciting, like all flirtations, by the eventual possibility of "doing something about it."

And meanwhile I listened to Gerald's ideas with growing enthusiasm. What appealed to me so strongly in his teaching was its lack of dogmatism. "Try it and find out for yourself" was, in effect, what he was telling me. Previously, I had thought of "religion" in terms of dogmas, commandments, and declarative statements—in terms, that is to say, of a Church. The Church presents its dogmatic ultimatum—"do this or be damned"—and you have to choose between accepting it in its entirety or rejecting it altogether. But what Gerald recommended was a practical mysticism, a do-it-yourself religion which was experimental and empirical. You were on your own, setting forth to find things out for yourself in your individual way. As a matter of historical fact, the Christian Church has always been somewhat unfriendly and suspicious in its attitude toward this kind of research, although it has been forced to admit from time to time that some of the researchers have been saints.

Gerald started out with a single proposition, which was actually no more than a working hypothesis: "The real self can be known." If you asked him what his authority was in making this statement, he would reply that it was the past experience of others—the great mystics such as Meister Eckhart, St. John of the Cross, and Ramakrishna, who had achieved this ultimate self-knowledge. (Gerald's conversation was full of such names— so many of them, indeed, that I never got the opportunity to find out who all of them were, especially since Gerald always courteously assumed that you knew. Ramakrishna's was one of the most frequently mentioned. I realized, of course, that he was an East Indian; beyond that, I was pretty vague, confusing him, more or less, with Krishnamurti [whom Gerald and Huxley knew personally] and with Radhakrishnan, the great scholar who was later to become president of India!)

But Gerald was quick to add that he wasn't asking you to take anything on trust. It was essential to try "this thing" for yourself. If, after a reasonable time, you had found nothing, then you were entitled to say that it was all a lie—and that the great mystics were madmen or hypocrites. This was his challenge, and it seemed to me that nothing could be fairer. In my excitement and enthusiasm, I kept asking: why didn't anybody ever tell me this before? The question was, of course, unreasonable. I had been "told this" innumerable times. Every moment of my waking life had contained within itself this riddle "what is life for?" and its answer "to learn what life means." Every event, every person I had met, had presented or indirectly stated both question and answer in some new way. Only, I hadn't been ready to listen. Why I was no ready—despite all my laziness and hesitations—I have just tried to explain.

I was ready, but I think I might still have procrastinated for a long time, if it hadn't been for the pressure of outside events. "The sheer beastliness of the world," as Gerald had called it, became increasingly obvious as the summer advanced and the hope of peace grew smaller. It was a ghastly time for everybody—except I suppose for those who actually wanted the war to come. Like the millions of others who didn't, I felt sick with foreboding. I didn't know how the crisis would affect my own life or what I was going to do about it, but I did know that I must find some kind of strength and belief within myself. I couldn't face what was coming in a state of agnostic stoicism. Only the very brave can be stoics, and even they often end in suicide.

At length, toward the end of July, I asked Gerald to take me to visit Swami Prabhavananda. I had decided to ask the swami to teach me meditation.

(The title of "swami" has more or less the same significance as that of "father" in the Catholic church, and it can only be properly assumed by a bona fide Hindu monk. The vast majority of those who call themselves swamis in this country— fortune-tellers, mental healers and the like—have absolutely no right to do so. At the time of his initiation, the swami receives a new Sanskrit name. "Prabhavananda" means "one who finds bliss within the Source of all creation." "Ananda," meaning "bliss" or "peace," as the suffix usually attached to a swami's name.)

The swami's home was in the hills above Hollywood. Although Hollywood Boulevard was only a few minutes' walk away, at the bottom of a steep hill, his street was then a very quiet one. (It has since been cut across by the freeway.) The swami lived in a pleasant old wooden house on the corner. Right next door to this house was a squat white plaster Hindu temple, surmounted by three onion-shaped domes whose pinnacles were painted gold. The temple stood at the top of two flights of brick steps, flanked by cypresses. The proportions of this layout were good; though so small, it was impressive.

The swami, also, I found to be small and impressive. Not formidable. Not in the least severe or hypnotic or dignified. But very definitely and unobtrusively one who had the authority of personal experience. Outwardly, he was a Bengali in his middle forties who looked at least fifteen years younger, charming and boyish in manner, with bold straight eyebrows and dark wide-set eyes. He talked in a gentle, persuasive voice. His smile was extraordinary—so open, so brilliant with joy that it had a strange kind of poignancy which could make your eyes fill suddenly with tears. Later, I got to know another look of his— an introspective look which seemed to withdraw all life from the surface of his face, leaving it quite bare and lonely, like the face of a mountain.

During our first interview, I felt terribly awkward. Everything I said sounded artificial. I started acting a little scene, trying to make myself appear sympathetic to him. I told him I wasn't sure that I could meditate and at the same time lead a life in "the world," earning my living writing movie scripts. He answered: "You must be like the lotus on the pond. The lotus leaf is never wet."

I said I was afraid of attempting to do too much, because I should be so discouraged if I failed. He said: "There is no failure in the search for God. Every step you take is a positive advance."

I said I hated the word *God*. He agreed that you could just as well say "The Self."

I asked how one could be sure that meditation wasn't just a process of autohypnosis. He replied: "Autohypnosis or auto-suggestion makes you see what you want to see. Meditation makes you see something you don't expect to see. Autosuggestion produces different results in each individual. Meditation produces the same result in all individuals."

I told him that I had always thought of such practices as nothing but a lot of mumbo jumbo. He laughed: "And now you have fallen into the trap?"

I don't think he was exactly bored by all this, only quietly aware of the futility of talk, at this point in the proceedings. So he waited, patiently and politely, for my chattering to end. As soon as I had taken at least one tiny step by myself, we would be able to talk practice instead of theory.

The swami's first instructions to me were, briefly, as follows:

1. Try to feel, all around you, the presence of an all-pervading Existence.
2. Send thoughts of peace and goodwill toward all beings—transmitting these thoughts consciously toward the four points of the compass in turn: north, south, east, and west.
3. Think of your own body as a temple which contains the Real Self, the Reality, which is infinite existence, infinite knowledge and infinite peace. (The Sanskrit words used to describe the nature of the Reality are *sat-chit-ananda*. The Reality does not have *sat* (existence), it *is* existence. It is also *chit*, consciousness; that is to say, it is all knowledge. It is also *ananda*, peace; the word I have already referred to, at the beginning of this chapter. *Ananda* is the peace of the spirit—in Christian language, "the peace of God which passeth all understanding." *Ananda* may also be translated as "bliss"; because absolute peace, independent of all change and circumstance, is the only genuine happiness.)
4. The Reality in yourself is the Reality within all other beings.

To sum up: this plan of meditation was a three-stage process. You sent your thoughts outward to the surrounding world, drew them inward upon yourself, then sent them outward again—but with a difference; for now you were no longer thinking of your fellow creatures as mere individuals but as temples containing the Reality. As mortal beings, you had offered them your goodwill; as the Eternal, you now offered them your reverence.

I have described all this in detail in order to illustrate an important point: these first instructions given me by the swami had no reference to the cult of any personal God-figure or divine incarnation. The assumptions they contained—that the Reality exists and can be contacted and known—were nondualistic assumptions. Knowledge of the Reality, in this context, means unitive knowledge—i.e. the realization that you, essentially, *are* the Reality, always were the Reality, and always will be. Where, then does the personal God-figure fit into this philosophy? Is there a place for him at all?

Yes, there is. The dualistic God—the God-who-is-other-than-I—is an aspect of the Reality but not other than the Reality. Within the world of phenomena—the world of a-partness, of this and that, of we and you—the God-who-is-other-than-we is the greatest phenomenon of all. But, with the experience of unitive, nondualistic knowledge, the God-who-is-other-than-I merges into the God-who-is-myself. The divine phenomena are seen to be all aspects of the one central Reality.

Let me deal with one simple misunderstanding which troubled me, and may trouble my readers. To say "I am God" is at one and the same time the most blasphemous statement you could possibly make, and also the truest. It all depends on what you mean by "I." If you mean, "my ego is God, Christopher Isherwood is God," then you are blaspheming; if you mean "my essential Self is God," then you are speaking the truth. It follows from this that you can never become one with the God-who-is-other-than-you—for "God" in this sense is also a projection of the central Reality. If you struggle, through meditation, for unitive knowledge of, let us say, Christ, there are two obstacles between you and its realization. One of them is your own individuality; the other is the individuality of Christ himself. If union is achieved, both these individualities must disappear; otherwise, the Reality within you cannot merge with the Reality within Christ.

This concept must naturally seem shocking to anyone who has been raised with a purely dualistic attitude to religion. And yet, for the nondualist, the dualistic approach to God seems altogether appropriate and, in many cases, preferable. It is almost impossible for me, in my average unregenerate state, to believe that I am a temple which contains the Reality. All I know of myself is my ego, and that appears to be a pretty squalid temple containing nothing of any value. So it is natural for me to turn toward some other being, one who really acts and speaks and appears as though the Reality were within him. By making a cult of this being—by adoring him and trying to resemble him—I can gradually come to an awareness of the Reality within myself. There you have the whole virtue of the cult.

The group for which Swami Prabhavananda was the leader was called officially The Vedanta Society of Southern California—a nonprofit religious corporation, established, in the words of its constitution, "to promote the study of the philosophy of Vedanta . . . and to promote harmony between Eastern and Western thought, and recognition of the truth in all the great religions of the world." (Vedanta means the philosophy which is taught in the Vedas—the most ancient of the Hindu scriptures. Thus one might say that Vedanta stands to yoga in the relation of theory to practice. Vedanta teaches us the nature of God and the universe. Yoga teaches us the ways in which union with God may be attained.)

When you first entered the temple of the Vedanta Society,

you might well be surprised by its plainness—especially if the curtains at the far end of it were drawn together. It was simply a lecture room, tastefully decorated in light gray, with comfortable rows of seats facing a kind of pulpit on a platform. On the walls were photographs of Ramakrishna, his wife (usually called the Holy Mother), his chief disciples Vivekananda and Brahmananda, together with a picture of an image of the Buddha and of the alleged head of Christ on the Turin shroud. There were no Hindu paintings or draperies or ornaments; nothing specifically Indian except for the Sanskrit word *Om,* which was carved on the pulpit. (Om is the word for God the Central Reality; it includes every deity, every aspect of the divine, but refers particularly to none. The word *Om* is chosen because it is thought to be the most comprehensive of all sounds, beginning back in the open throat and ending on the closed lips; and thus symbolizing God, the all-encompassing.)

Thus, when you first entered the temple, you didn't at all feel that you were caught in a religious spider's web. Being there didn't commit you to anything. You could sit down in a mood of objective curiosity and listen to one of the swami's Sunday lectures on Vedanta philosophy. The audience was not required to participate in any act of worship, either before or after the lectures. Nor, if you were a Christian, did you need to leave your beliefs at home. The swami always took it for granted that there would be many Christians among his hearers, and he constantly referred to Christ's teachings to illustrate the points he was making. In his eyes, Christ was one of the great spiritual teachers of mankind, to be spoken of with the deepest reverence. But this degree of recognition wouldn't, of course, have satisfied the orthodox Christian minister of any sect. For such a minister, the swami was still a heathen—even if an enlightened one—because he didn't admit that Christ was the *only* teacher, the *only* doorway to the truth.

But the temple had another aspect. It really *was* a temple, and not merely the lecture room of a philosophical society. When the curtains were drawn apart, you saw that there was a small windowless shrine room beyond the platform on which the pulpit stood. Within this shrine room, on a pedestal of two steps, stood the shrine itself. It had been made in India, of intricately carved, highly polished dark wood; four double corinthian pillars supporting a dome. This shrine was exposed to the full view of the audience during the swami's lectures. Decked with garlands of flowers and lit by candles in glass candlesticks with sparkling pendants, it looked magically pretty; and no doubt the casual visitor to the temple, who saw it from the distance of his seat in the lecture hall, thought of it merely as a charming and picturesque focal point in the scheme of decoration. As a matter of fact, it was the focal point of the whole life of the Vedanta Society.

For the society, as I gradually discovered, didn't only exist to propagate the study of Vedanta philosophy. That was only one half—the less important half—of its purpose. The major purpose of the society was to encourage its members to lead lives in which the search for the Reality was a central preoccupation and a matter of daily private practice, not just public Sunday observance. Even the busiest of them were expected to find time every day for meditation. Some actually had shrines in their own homes. Many were devotees of Ramakrishna as a divine incarnation; but Prabhavananda never insisted on this. If you preferred to meditate on Christ, or any other holy figure, or upon the impersonal God, then you were taught how to do so.

The swami himself belonged to an order of Indian monks called the Ramakrishna Order. It had been founded by Vivekananda, one of Ramakrishna's two chief disciples; the other, Brahmananda, had been the first head of the order and the guru (teacher) of Prabhavananda. So we in Hollywood might feel ourselves to be still very near to the fountainhead.

Under the dome of the shrine, a photograph of Ramakrishna occupied the central position. To the right of this was a photograph of Holy Mother; to the left were images of Buddha and

Krishna and a Russian icon of Christ. Photographs of Brahmananda and Vivekananda stood on the lower level, together with images of some other Hindu deities. Meditation periods, accompanied by ritual worship, were held in the shrine room three times a day by the swami and those members of the group who wished to take part in them. Though the swami taught all his pupils to meditate, he never said that they must take part, directly or indirectly, in the ritual worship. Ritual worship and indeed the whole cult of a divine personality, formed, according to his teaching, only one of the several ways, the yogas, to knowledge of the Reality. The swami told us that there was actually one monastery of the Ramakrishna Order—Mayavati in the Himalayas—at which there was no shrine and no ritual worship, in order that the monks might accustom themselves to meditating without these adjuncts.

It didn't take much experience of meditation in the shrine room—which I now visited whenever I had time—to bring home to me one self-evident fact: that a spiritual atmosphere—or indeed any other kind of an atmosphere—can be deliberately created. In this case, the atmosphere of the shrine room was extraordinarily calming, and yet *alive*. When you came into it, with your head full of the anxieties and preoccupations of the outside world, you found yourself relaxing almost at once: but not—as would have happened in any ordinary quiet place—into sleep. One of my friends said that it was like being in a wood; and this seemed to me a very apt description. Just as, in a wood, you can become aware that the trees are alive all around you, so I sometimes felt as if the shine room were filled with consciousness—the consciousness of all those who were meditating and had meditated in it.

But the shrine was something more than this. It was more than a kind of meditation bank, into which we had made deposits and which now paid interest. It was also a holy place, a living presence. Within the shrine were relics of Ramakrishna, Holy Mother, and their disciples. The Hindus believe—as the

Catholics believe—that such relics give forth power; that they generate spiritual radiations which can actually affect the lives of those who are exposed to them. The swami believed that, by virtue of the relics, Ramakrishna and the others were present within the shrine in a special sense; and that it was therefore absolutely necessary that the ritual worship should be performed before it every day.

My reactions to the temple and what it stood for can probably be imagined—both pro and con. (I have since found them to be the usual reactions of anyone who comes into contact with the Vedanta Society for the first time—always providing that he or she hasn't had previous dealings with Theosophy or some other system of metaphysics; in which case a different response pattern is set up.) On the con side, I was of course powerfully repelled by the specifically Indian aspects of the Ramakrishna cult. Why did the rituals in the shrine have to be Hindu rituals? Why did several of the women devotees like to wear saris in the shrine room? Why were the prayers in Sanskrit? Why did we so often have curry at meals?

I think these objections were rooted in a twofold prejudice. Whether I liked it or not, I had been brought up in the Christian tradition; anything outside that tradition repelled me as being unnecessarily alien. Also, as a member, whether I liked it or not, of the British upper class, I had somewhere deep inside me a built-in contempt for the culture of "native," "subject" races. If my subconscious had been allowed to speak out clearly, it would have said: "I quite admit that you have the truth, but does it have to come to me wearing a turban? Can't I be an Anglo-Saxon Vedantist?" In fact, it would have talked like Naaman the leper in the Bible story. Naaman had the greatest respect for Elisha. He believed that Elisha could cure him of his leprosy. But he hated to be told to wash himself in the river Jordan. "Are not Abana and Pharpar, rivers of Damascus, better than all the waters of Israel?" Aren't the Rhine and the Hudson better than the Ganges?

But, in my pro mood, I was easily able to answer these objections. In the first place, if you have made up your mind to worship God in a particular form, then obviously you have to start with the externals. You have to recognize the fact that Ramakrishna was an Indian and that Christ was a Jew (a fact, incidentally, which many Christians try hard to forget). Lack of documentation permits the Christian to imagine Christ's physical appearance more or less as he likes. Of Ramakrishna we have photographs.

Having pictured the man, you next have to picture his surroundings: the place he lived in, the clothes he wore, the food he ate, the kind of people and events which would fill his exterior everyday life. It is most important to do this, because you then have to try to fit yourself into the scene; to approach Ramakrishna in his own proper setting, asking yourself, "Should *I* have recognized him, then, for what he really was?"

When you think of the problem in this way, it is easy to see the value of these Indian accessories; to see why you should perform the same rituals which Ramakrishna himself used to perform, as a young priest; why you should say prayers and chant chants in the language that he spoke; why, while you are trying to meditate upon him, you should wear the chadars or saris which are native to his country; why, even, you should eat the food that he ate.

And so the seesaw of reactions goes back and forth. The devotee does not want to turn himself into a kind of synthetic Hindu—no; that would be ridiculous and anyhow impossible. But he does want to get as close to the personality of Ramakrishna as he can; even on the external level. So the Indianness alternately repels and attracts him. That, at least, was my own experience. Luckily for me and for the many others who felt as I did, Swami Prabhavananda had a deeply sympathetic and often humorous understanding of our difficulty. Indeed, it was this understanding which set the whole tone of life in the small household which was then the nucleus of the Vedanta Society.

And now I should say something about the Society itself: how and why it started.

In 1886, immediately after Ramakrishna's death in Calcutta, the inner ring of disciples, led by Vivekananda and Brahmananda, bound themselves together by taking *sannyas,* the final monastic vow. They did not, however, immediately form an official monastic order.

In 1893, Vivekananda came to America to attend a Parliament of Religions which was being held as part of the Columbian Exposition in Chicago. Although Vivekananda was unknown and was not an official delegate—his traveling expenses had been scraped together with great difficulty—his success as a speaker was enormous. At the end of the Parliament's session, he was asked to visit many cities in the States and to found centers in which the teaching of Vedanta could be continued.

In 1897, after Vivekananda's return to India, he and his brother monks conferred together and put the activities of the Ramakrishna Order on an organized basis. First, a mission was founded; then, two years later, a math (monastery). The headquarters of both math and mission are at Belur, just outside Calcutta; branch centers have gradually been opened all over India. The mission is primarily active in social work, running schools and hospitals and administering famine or epidemic relief projects; the math is primarily active in the training of monks and in ritual worship. But the two are not really separate entities, except for the convenience of planning and the allotment of funds. Swamis of the order keep exchanging one way of life for the other: spending some time in meditation and solitude, then taking on administrative duties at one of the mission centers.

In 1899, Vivekananda came back to the United States. This time, he was chiefly occupied in forming centers and training devotees. He arranged for swamis of the Ramakrishna Order to come over from India and take charge of these centers.

In the early part of 1900, during this visit, Vivekananda spent six weeks at the house of three sisters who lived in Pasadena, California. One of these was Mrs. Carrie Mead Wyckoff, a widow. Vivekananda returned to India and died in 1902, but Mrs. Wyckoff never lost touch with the Ramakrishna Order. She met two other direct disciples of Ramakrishna, Swamis Turiyananda and Trigunatita, both of whom came to America to supervise the San Francisco Vedanta center. Swami Trigunatita gave her a Sanskrit name-in-religion; this was a usual practice among the devotees of the order. He called her Sister Lalita (Lalita was one of the handmaidens of Krishna), and it was as "Sister" that she was always known at the time when I met her.

In 1928, Sister met Swami Prabhavananda. He had been sent to the States five years previously, as assistant to Swami Prakashananda who was then the head of the San Francisco Center. Later he had founded a Vedanta Society in Portland, Oregon, at the request of some devotees of Ramakrishna who were living there.

In 1929, Sister invited Prabhavananda to come down to Los Angeles, and she put her modest house and income at the disposal of the future Vedanta Society of Southern California. At first, it was a very small society indeed. An Englishwoman whom they called Amiya came to keep house for the elderly lady and the youthful monk; after a while, they were joined by two or three others. The swami's lectures were given in the living room, and it was quite big enough to hold his tiny audience. Financially speaking, they lived from week to week. The swami often did the cooking. Going to the movies was an occasional and special treat. Nevertheless, they seem to have had a great deal of fun.

Then, around 1936, the congregation began to expand considerably. Prabhavananda became locally well known as a speaker and respected as an individual. It was now only rarely that anyone would telephone to ask if the swami would draw up a horoscope or give a public performance of his yoga powers. In fact, word had got around that this *wasn't* a swami in the usual California sense. And now enough money was donated to build a temple. Sister's house had already been enlarged to include a shrine room, but this was much too small; and the living room was no longer big enough for the lectures. Finding a site for the temple presented no problem, for there was room in Sister's garden. So the work went ahead; and the temple was completed and dedicated in July 1938, about a year before I first set eyes on it.

But although the society was steadily growing—although quite a lot of people came to hear Swami speak on Sundays, and even more to hear Gerald Heard, who sometimes took his place—the group in Sister's house was still very much a family. "The Lord's Family," the swami called it; and you really did feel, even as an outside visitor, that Ramakrishna was established in that household, that he presided over it in a curiously intimate, domestic manner. There was no dividing line between the activities of the temple and the daily life of the group. Cooking and even eating the lunch was actually all part of the ritual worship, since a portion of what you were going to eat was first offered to the Lord during the worship in the shrine room and then brought back and mixed in with the rest of the food, thus consecrating the entire meal and making it sacramental. And, as the inevitable result of all this going and coming between shrine and kitchen, the women of the household had lost any sense of "sacred" and "profane." They carried their jokes back and forth between the Eternal and the temporal; cooking disasters and mistakes in the ritual were discussed at table in exactly the same tone of voice and with the same amount of amusement. Yes, there were times when all this

Hinduism seemed sticky and theatrical and cloyingly sentimental. But it certainly brought Ramakrishna close to you—it was almost shamelessly cozy—and oh, I used to think to myself, oh, my goodness, what a relief from the reverent stuffiness of the Sunday religion I had been brought up in!

In the late autumn of 1940, when I had been coming to the Vedanta Society for about fifteen months, Prabhavananda decided to initiate me. The ceremony of initiation is standard Hindu practice: it consists, essentially, in the giving of a mantra by the guru to his disciple. The word *mantra* cannot be exactly translated into English, though the idea it expresses is not foreign to the Christian tradition. The mantra consists of several holy names, which the disciple is to repeat and meditate upon, for the rest of his life. It is regarded as very sacred and very private. You must never tell your mantra to any other human being. The act of repeating it is called *japa*. Because one usually resolves to make a certain fixed amount of japa every day, it is convenient to use a rosary. The rosary serves to measure the japa—one bead to each repetition of the mantra— so that you are not distracted by having to count.

The ceremony of initiation was necessarily a simple one, since it had to be repeated several times. Prabhavananda would usually initiate four or five people on the same day. The day chosen would be one of our special festivals; this one was the birthday of the Holy Mother.

The initiation took place before breakfast, right after the first of the day's three meditation periods. Before going into the temple, I was provided by one of the women of the family with a small tray on which were arranged the flowers I was to offer: two red roses, a white rose, and a large daisy. The swami was waiting for me inside the shrine; its curtains had been drawn for privacy. First, he told me to offer the flowers: to the photographs of Ramakrishna and Holy Mother, to the icon of

Christ, and to himself—because the guru must always receive at least a token of an initiation gift. Next, he taught me my mantra, making me repeat it several times until I was quite sure of it. Next, he gave me a rosary and showed me how to use it. (The Hindu rosaries are made of small dried seeds which come from the East Indian islands, strung on a silk thread. There are 108 beads, plus a lead bead with a tassel attached to it. When you are "telling" the beads, you never make a complete rotation because, when you come to the tassel-bead, you reverse the rosary and start it the other way around. The tassel-bead is said to represent the guru. Out of the hundred and eight repetitions of the mantra which make up one rotation, one hundred are said to be for your own devotions and the other eight are made on behalf of the rest of mankind. These latter represent a labor of love and are therefore not counted; so, for the purposes of reckoning how much japa you intend to make daily, you count each rotation of the rosary as one hundred only. I suppose the average amount of japa made by an energetic devotee would be between five and ten thousand a day.)

With my initiation, I entered into a kind of relationship which will seem hopelessly strange or perhaps quite incomprehensible to many of my readers. I mean the relationship between guru and disciple. It is not that I am trying to sound mysteriously impressive or that I am laying claim to any great mystical experience. Indeed, I do not pretend to understand much about this relationship myself.

In India, the guru-disciple relationship is regarded as being of the greatest possible importance. It is essential to find yourself a guru, because your guru is the nearest link in a chain which connects you with one of the great spiritual teachers and hence with direct knowledge of God. This chain is a spiritual lifeline to all who can grasp hold of it. It is in this sense that the Hindu scriptures declare: "The Guru is God."

Having found your guru, you must now persuade him to initiate you; for it is only with initiation that the relationship can properly be said to have begun. But the guru may well hesitate before agreeing to this, because, in accepting a new disciple, he is taking on yet another tremendous responsibility. According to Hindu belief, the tie between guru and disciple can never be broken, either in this world or any other. It survives death, separation, estrangement, and even downright betrayal. In other words, there would be no way for a Christ to disown a Judas.

The mantra is the guru's greatest gift to his disciple. It is, as it were, the essence of his teaching and of himself. By virtue of the mantra, the guru is present with the disciple at all times, no matter how far they may be apart. And just as the guru is the link in a physical chain of teachers, so the mantra is a link in a spiritual chain which corresponds to it.

What is more, the mantra always contains one or more "seed-words," as they are called. (The chief of these is the word *Om*, which I have already referred to.) These seed-words are regarded by the Hindus as being infinitely more than just words. They actually contain God's presence. Here, at least, is a concept which should not seem strange to Western minds. Every Christian knows how the gospel according to John begins: "In the beginning was the Word, and the Word was with God, and the Word was God." What very, very few Christians know is that they could find in the Rig Veda, one of the Hindu scriptures which dates from many centuries earlier, a verse: "In the beginning was Brahman, with whom was the Word; and the Word was truly the supreme Brahman" (i.e. the transcendent Reality). Seed-words are no longer employed by Christians, it is true. But the Catholics do use rosaries and make what corresponds to japa. "Hail Mary" is a form of mantra. And, in the teachings of the Greek Orthodox Church, we find that a prayer of constant repetition is recommended, the prayer in this case being "Lord Jesus Christ, have mercy on me."

As to the efficacy of such a prayer, it is only necessary to tell the reader to try it. No amount of mockery or argument will ever prove anything to him, either way. It is like the symbolic pump handle in Tolstoy's *A Confession*. If you move it up and down, you may get water. If you deny that it *is* a pump handle and refuse even to try it, then you most certainly never will.

At the Vedanta Society, we had always before us the example of a guru-disciple relationship which really generated power. I have said that Swami Prabhavanada was a disciple of Brahmananda. Brahmananda had died in 1922, and Prabhavananda had not even seen so very much of his guru while he was alive; for Brahmananda had many duties as head of the order and had had to travel constantly from one monastery to another. And yet Brahmananda had been, and still was, the one dominant figure in Prabhavananda's life. He told us with absolute sincerity that he believed Brahmananda had all of us in his charge; that Brahmananda was personally directing the development of our society. Whatever any of us might think of these statements, we couldn't doubt that the swami not only meant them but also—which was far more impressive—led his own life *as if* they were true. He really did have the air of a second-in-command, and this attitude gave him a fundamental lack of vanity. I soon came to realize this and to respect it.

This lack of vanity was demonstrated by Swami's firm refusal to try to make an impression on those who met him. For example, quite a number of people were shocked by his chain-smoking of cigarettes. Horrors—you thought at first—an addiction! Later, you began to ask yourself if you would really have preferred to have a guru without weaknesses. How could one love, or even admire, such a creature? (As a matter of fact, many years later, Prabhavananda suddenly and completely gave up smoking—not on moral grounds but because the doctor told him to.)

The question may well be asked: what if the guru I find for myself is a bad man, a hypocrite, a pretender? The answer to this seems to be: if you pick the wrong guru, you will only have yourself to blame. This may sound rather heartless; but it is impossible, on the other hand, not to agree that the many gullible rich women of this country who make possible the existence of fake religions are quite as guilty as the false prophets who run them. The Hindu idea is that you should subject your prospective guru to every kind of test, until you are entirely convinced of his honesty. Then, and only then, should you submit your will to him and obey him absolutely. At the same time, it may be said as a consolation to the unwise that a bad guru is not a dead loss. The Catholics believe that the sacraments administered by an morally bad priest are still valid. The Hindus believe that a mantra given by a morally bad swami is still valid. The chain of spiritual power remains unbroken.

Finally there comes the question: how will I set about finding a guru? To this the Hindus answer: when you really need a guru, you will find one. This is one of the many statements about religious matters which I must—in Gerald Heard's phrase—"put into my suspense account." I don't say I don't believe it; but, in my present stage of ignorance, I have no way of finding out if it is true. That it has been true in my own case is evident. That it is true universally, I would like to believe—if only because the alternative seems to be a Calvinistic smugness. You are never in deadlier danger than when you believe you have been individually "chosen" and "saved."

PART II

WHAT IS VEDANTA?

What Is Vedanta?

First of all, what is Vedanta?

Vedanta is a philosophy evolved from the Vedas, those Indian scriptures which are the most ancient religious writings now known to the world. More generally speaking, the term *Vedanta* covers not only the Vedas themselves but the whole mass of literature which explains their teaching. The Bhagavad Gita and the works of Shankara belong to Vedanta.

Vedanta is often, but less correctly, called "Hinduism," a foreign word. The inhabitants of India were described by the Persians as "Hindus," because they lived on the other side of the River Shindhu, or Indus. The Persians could not manage the sound of the letter *s*.

In India today, as elsewhere, there are hundreds of sects. Vedanta philosophy is the basis of them all. Indeed, in its simplest form, it may be said to be the equivalent of the Philosophia Perennis; the least common denominator of all religious belief.

Reduced to its elements, Vedanta philosophy consists of three principles. First, that man's real nature is divine. Second, that the aim of human life is to realize this divinity. Third, that truth is universal. We shall examine each of them in turn.

Man's real nature is divine: what does this actually mean? Vedanta asserts that the universe which is perceived by our senses is only an appearance. It is not what it seems. Here, the modern scientist will, of course, agree. Who would ever suppose, in looking at a flower, a rock, and a waterfall, that each was merely an arrangement of identical units, with its own peculiar atomic structure? The universe is other than its outward aspect; and even this outward aspect is subject to perpetual change. The hills, said Tennyson, are shadows.

Vedanta asserts that, beneath this appearance, this flux, there is an essential, unchanging Reality, which it calls Brahman, the Godhead. Brahman is Existence itself, Consciousness itself. Brahman is also said to be that almost indefinable quality which is called in the Sanskrit language "Ananda," and in the Christian Bible "the peace which passeth all understanding." "Ananda" is translated not only as "peace" but also as "bliss"; since this absolute peace, when it is known within all flux, appearance, and unrest, must give the only permanent kind of happiness.

At the mention of Brahman, the modern scientist will become skeptical, or at least agnostic. And rightly so, for none of his apparatus is capable of detecting the existence of this fundamental Reality. Vedanta will reply that the scientist cannot possibly detect Brahman, because scientific analysis depends, necessarily, upon the evidence of the five senses, and Brahman is beyond all sense perception. Why, it will be asked, should we believe with Vedanta instead of doubting with the scientist? But the answer to this question must be delayed for a moment, until we begin to discuss the nature of the mystical experience.

Let us assume, in the meanwhile, that Brahman does exist. If there is indeed an essential Reality, a Godhead, in the universe, then it follows that this Reality must be omnipresent. It must be within each one of us; within every creature and object. It does not matter exactly what we mean by "within": that is a point for theologians to argue. Let us say simply, at the risk of offending the exponents of semantics, that Brahman is our real, essential nature. When speaking of Brahman-within, Vedanta uses, for convenience, another Sanskrit term, "the Atman." The Atman, in Christian terminology, is God Immanent; Brahman is God Transcendent. But Atman and Brahman are one.

And now, with the second of the Vedanta principles, we

come to most of our difficulties. The aim of human life, we are told, is to realize the Atman, our essential nature.

Why? How? Who says so? How does he know?

In the first place, why? The answer to this question is by no means evident to the majority of people alive on earth today. Human life has many apparent aims: we have only to read the advertisements in the daily paper to realize that. Win the war. Win the peace. Get your man. Get a home. Get a better job. Become beautiful. Become a good speaker. Read the hundred best books. Avoid a thousand common mistakes in speaking English. Learn a foreign language in a month. Such are our objectives. And millions strive for them, with the greatest earnestness, courage, and devotion, day after day.

To seek to realize my essential nature is to admit that I am dissatisfied with my nature as it is at present. It is to admit that I am dissatisfied with the life I am leading now. But am I? The lovers in each other's arms, the successful politician on election night, the financier who has just brought off a big deal (not to mention the great mass of normally healthy, well-adjusted men and women absorbed in their families and their work) will at once protest: "Leave us alone. We are doing very nicely as we are."

"Are you? We doubt it," says Buddha, Jesus, Shankara, Shakespeare, and Tolstoy. And they proceed to point out, in their different languages and styles, that death brings an end to all desire, that worldly wealth is a house built upon the sand, that the beautiful body is a vessel of filth and decay, that ambition will be pricked like an inflated bladder, that our bustling activity resembles the fever of patients in a madhouse. Their words depress us; for the truth is obvious, if we consider it. But we do not wish to consider it. The dinner will boil over. We are late already for that appointment. So we dismiss our prophets as pessimists and hurry away with a sigh, resolved to have a good time while we can, or, at any rate, to get on with the next job.

But suppose I really am dissatisfied. I am tired, I am bored, I am puzzled. The world fails to answer my questions. Suppose I am ready to assume, provisionally, that this Atman, this essential nature, does exist within me, and does offer a lasting strength, wisdom, peace, and happiness. How am I to realize that nature? How am I to enjoy it?

The answer is given, unanimously, by all the teachers and prophets. It is very disconcerting:

"By ceasing to be yourself."

"What do you mean? That's nonsense. How can I stop being myself? I'm Christopher Isherwood, or I'm nothing."

"You aren't really Christopher Isherwood. You're the Atman."

"Then why do I think I'm myself?"

"Because of your ignorance. Christopher Isherwood is only an appearance, a part of the apparent universe. He is a constellation of desires and impulses. He reflects his environment. He repeats what he has been taught. He mimics the social behavior of his community. He copies gestures like a monkey and intonations like a parrot. All his actions are conditioned by those around him, however individual and eccentric they may seem to be. He is subject to suggestion, climate, and the influence of drugs. He is changing all the time. He has no essential reality."

"But why do I identify myself with him, if I'm really the Atman? How did this ignorance start? What caused it?"

Here, the prophets will give slightly different answers. Buddha will refuse to discuss the subject at all, saying that it is not important. When the house is burning, does it matter if the man who fired it had red hair? It is only necessary that we should realize that the house *is* burning. Or, to put it more mildly, that we should be dissatisfied with our present condition and ready to do something about it.

Christian theology will speak of original sin and postulate a fall of man from consciousness of his divine nature. Vedanta does not accept this idea. It conceives of a universe coexistent with Brahman, equally beginningless and endless. Even if the universe should be apparently destroyed, it will only have gone back into a kind of seed-state, a phase of potentiality, from which, in due time, it will reemerge. Vedanta teaches that the stuff of this universe is an effect or power of Brahman. It stands to Brahman in the same relation as heat to fire. They are inseparable. Brahman does not intervene amidst these phenomena. The question "why does God permit evil?" is, to a Vedantist, as meaningless as "why does God permit good?" The fire warms one man and burns another and is neither kind nor cruel.

An inhuman philosophy? Certainly. Brahman is not human. We must beware of thinking about the Reality in human terms. It is not simply a giant person. It has nothing to do with our relative standards of good and evil, pleasant and unpleasant, right and wrong.

But let us return to our dialogue:

"All right. We'll forget about the cause of ignorance. Now how do I stop being Christopher Isherwood?"

"By ceasing to believe that you are. What is this belief? Egotism, nothing else. An egotism which is asserted and reinforced by hundreds of your daily actions. Every time you desire or fear or hate, every time you boast or indulge your vanity, every time you struggle to get something for yourself, you are really asserting: 'I am Christopher Isherwood. I am separate from everything else in this universe. I am a private, unique individual.' But you aren't, you know. The scientist will agree with me that you aren't. Every creature and object in this world is interrelated; biologically, psychologically, physically, politically, economically. They are all of a piece."

"So the only thing I have to do is stop believing I'm an individual?"

"It isn't so easy. First, you must start acting as though you had ceased to believe it. Try to overcome this possessive attitude toward your actions. Stop taking credit for your successes. Stop bemoaning your failures, or making excuses for them.

Stop worrying so much about results. Just go on doing your best. Work for the work's sake. Think of your body, if you like, as an instrument."

"Whose instrument?"

"The instrument of the Atman."

"Why should I work for the Atman? It doesn't need my help."

"There is no question of helping the Atman. All action done in this spirit is symbolic. It becomes a form of worship."

"How dull that sounds! Where's the inducement? What's the motive?"

"Love."

"You mean, I should love the Atman? How can I?"

"You love Christopher Isherwood, don't you?"

"Yes, I suppose so. Most of the time. When I don't hate him."

"Then you ought to love your real self much more. The Atman is perfect. Christopher Isherwood isn't."

"But I know him. I've never seen the Atman. I'm not even sure it exists."

"Try to feel that it exists. Think about it. Pray to it. Meditate on it. Know that you are it."

"You mean, hypnotize myself."

"If it's nothing but autohypnosis, you'll soon find out. Hypnosis wouldn't give you any permanent results. It wouldn't give you the peace and strength and understanding you are looking for. It wouldn't help you to accept life. It wouldn't transform your character. Neither would drink, for that matter, or dope. I'm only asking you to try it. This is a matter for experiment."

"Very well. What else am I to do?"

"Judge every thought and every action from this standpoint: does it make me freer, less egotistic, more aware of the Reality; or does it attach me more tightly to Christopher Isherwood? I don't want to use the word *sin*. Let's call them obstructions.

You'll find, in practice, that certain thoughts and actions obstruct your progress. Give them up. Other thoughts and actions will assist your progress. Cultivate them."

"Tell me some."

"Chastity, truthfulness, generosity, not injuring others."

"Chastity? I'm to give up sex?"

"You'll find you have to, in the end."

"Why? It's not wrong."

"I never said it was. But what does it lead to? Attachment to this world of appearance. An added conviction that you're Christopher Isherwood."

"Oh, you just hate the world, that's all!"

"It's you who hate the world, in your heart of hearts. You are bound to hate it, because you know only its appearance, and its appearance seems to end in death. But I see the Reality within the appearance. I see the world within Reality. And I love it as I love the Reality itself."

"I must say, all this sounds very selfish. I'm to spend the rest of my life trying to know my real nature. Thinking about myself, in fact. What about my neighbors? Am I to forget them altogether? What about my duty to the community? What about social service?"

"From the first moment you start trying to know your real nature and acting in the way I have shown you, your life will be nothing but social service. You will be more available to your neighbors than ever before, because you will be less egotistic. You will do your duty to the community far better, because your motives will be less mixed with vanity and the wish for power and self-advertisement. You think you love some of your neighbors now. You cannot dream how you will love them all, when you begin to see the Reality within every human being. What is it that your neighbors need most? Isn't it just that strength, that reassurance, that knowledge and peace which are the objects of your search? How can you transmit them to others, until you have won them for yourself? By helping yourself, you are helping them. By helping them, you are helping your-self. That's the law of all spiritual progress."

"Provided, of course, that the Reality exists."

"The Reality does exist."

"How do you know?"

"Because I have experienced it."

"Why should I believe you?"

"Because I tell you so. Because you can experience it yourself."

There we have it, our greatest difficulty. There the scientist cannot help us. He only shrugs his shoulders and says "per-haps." The prophet tells us that he has seen God, and we have each of us to make up our minds whether to believe him or not. (I have discussed this question more fully in my article "Hypothesis and Belief.")

In order to be able to decide whether the prophet is telling the truth or lying, we shall have to investigate the mystical experience for ourselves. This can be done in two ways: from the outside, by studying the biographies and writings of the saints; and from the inside, by following the instructions they have given us. To follow these instructions is to lead what Christians call "the unitive life." In Sanskrit, the word for this unitive life is *yoga,* from which is derived our English word *yoke,* or union. Yoga is the technique of union with the Atman.

However we may choose to explain it, the historical fact remains that thousands of men and women, belonging to every century, country, and social class, have attempted, with apparent success, to follow this way of life. According to the evidence of their contemporaries, they have undergone that slow strange transformation, that inner process of readjustment, which ends in what is called sainthood. Hundreds of them, Christian, Ve-dantist, Buddhist, Taoist, Sufi, and Jew, have left records of their experience; and these records show remarkable similarity. Some are devotional in the extreme: they worship the Reality in human form, a Krishna, a Rama, a Christ, with ecstasies of love. Some meditate on the impersonal Brahman, with the seeming coldness of pure discrimination, bowing before no altar or image. Some have visions. Some have powers over material nature and can heal the sick. Some live in caves or cells. Some in crowded cities. Some are great orators. Some refuse to utter a word. Some are laughed at and believed to be mad. Some are respected for their qualities of clear judgment and sanity. Some are martyred.

It is upon the nature of the supreme mystical experience that all agree. What is this experience? It seems that when the ego-sense has, through constant self-discipline, grown very weak, there comes a moment (it is often the moment of death) at which the presence of the essential nature is no longer concealed. The saint becomes aware that the Atman actually does exist. Further, he experiences the nature of the Atman as his own nature. He knows he is nothing but Reality. This is what Christian writers call "the mystic union" and Vedantists "samadhi."

We have been told that the Reality is beyond sense perception. How, then, can it be experienced? This is a very difficult question; perhaps it cannot be answered in words. Samadhi is said to be a fourth kind of consciousness: it is beyond the states of waking, dreaming, and dreamless sleep. Those who have witnessed it as an external phenomenon, report that the experiencer appeared to have fallen into a kind of trance. The hair of the head and body stood erect. The half-closed eyes became fixed. Sometimes there was an astonishing loss of weight, or even levitation of the body from the ground. But these are mere symptoms and tell us nothing. There is only one way to find out what samadhi is like: you must have it yourself.

Vedanta's third principle, that truth is universal, needs less discussion. But it is psychologically very important. Being a philosophy rather than a religion, Vedanta is not sectarian and therefore not exclusive. It appeals, as it were, over the heads of the sectarians and dogmatists, to the practicing mystics of all religions. Also, by classifying the sects themselves as different paths of yoga all leading to the same goal, it seeks to establish a sort of religious synthesis. Tolerance is, in any case, natural to the Indian temperament. But, unfortunately, it cannot be claimed that this unifying effort has, so far, been very successful. Vedanta may accept Christ as the Son of God. It may acknowledge Allah. But Christians and Muslims persist in regarding their respective religions as the only true faith. Christian and Sufi mystics have been compelled, by the very nature of their mystical experience, to take a more liberal attitude. In consequence, they have often been suspected of heresy and sometimes actually condemned by their coreligionists.

Nor does the Vedantist, in expressing his reverence for Allah and Christ, mean quite what orthodox Muslims and Christians would like him to mean. Vedanta, as I have said already, offers a philosophical basis to all sects. It can do this precisely because it is fundamentally monistic; because it teaches that there is one Reality and nothing else. "Thou art That." The person is the Atman; the Atman is Brahman. This person in his ignorance, may think that he worships the Creator. Very well: let him think that. It is a necessary stage in spiritual progress. The ultimate truth cannot be apprehended at once. The Atman must be personified at first, if it is to be loved and realized; otherwise it will remain a mere intellectual abstraction. The true monist never disdains dualism. But it is very hard for the rigid dualist ever to accept monism. St. Ignatius Loyola was dismayed when the vision of his beloved Jesus faded into the impersonal, all-embracing Reality.

The Indian mind, because it is fundamentally monistic, has no difficulty in believing that the one impersonal Brahman may have an infinite number of personal aspects. As many, indeed, as there are worshipers; since an aspect is literally a view, and each traveler may see a different angle of a mountain. These aspects are represented in Indian art, sculpture, and literature with such a wealth of form and attribute that the Western foreigner (whose religious mentality is dualistic) is apt to mistake them for gods and goddesses in the pagan sense, and to exclaim indignantly that this is polytheism. Hence, much misunderstanding arises. Here, in the West, we have a dualistic religion and a monistic science, in apparent conflict with each other. And so, paradoxically enough, it is comparatively easy for a scientist to accept Vedanta, and extremely hard for a Christian to do so.

According to Vedanta, the Reality may also take human form and enter the world, from time to time. Why it should do this is a mystery which no amount of philosophical analysis can solve. It is the paradox which we call grace, expressed in its most startling terms. The Reality is manifested, occasionally, amidst the temporal appearance. Brahman *does,* after all, sometimes intervene. As Sri Krishna says in the Gita:

> In every age I come back
> To deliver the holy,
> To destroy the sin of the sinner,
> To establish righteousness.

The Vedantist calls such incarnations of the Reality "avatars." He recognizes Rama, Krishna, Buddha, and Christ as avatars, along with several others, and believes that there will be many more. But the Christian, convinced of the uniqueness of Christ as a spiritual phenomenon, can hardly be expected to subscribe to this belief.

After samadhi, what? What happens to the few who attain it, and to the hundreds of millions who don't?

This brings us to the hypothesis of karma and reincarnation. I use the word *hypothesis* deliberately, because I am writing for Western and, I hope, intelligently skeptical readers. It is my business to describe, not to dogmatize. Here is one explanation of the known facts of our human experience. You can accept or reject it. But, unless you understand its main propositions, the literature of Vedanta will scarcely be intelligible to you. *Karma* means action, work, a deed. Not only physical action, conscious or reflex, but also mental action, conscious or subconscious. Karma is everything that we think or do. Philosophically speaking, karma also means the law of causation: a law which is said to operate not only in the physical, but also in the mental and moral sphere of our lives.

I do an action; I think a thought. The Vedantist tells me that this action and this thought, even though they be apparently over and done with, will inevitably, sooner or later, produce some effect. This effect may be pleasant, or unpleasant, or a mixture of both. It may be long delayed. I may never notice it. I may have altogether forgotten the action or the thought which caused it. Nevertheless, it will be produced.

Furthermore, every action and every thought makes an impression upon the mind. This impression may be slight, at first; but, if the same action or thought is repeated, it will deepen into a kind of groove, down which our future behavior will easily tend to run. These mental grooves we call our tendencies. Their existence makes it possible to predict fairly accurately just how each of us will behave in any given situation. In other words, the sum of our karmas represents our character. As fresh karmas are added and previous karmas exhausted or neutralized, our character changes.

So much is self-evident. But now comes the question: where does karma begin? Are we all born equal? Do we all start life with the same chances of failure and success? Why Shakespeare? Why the mongolian idiot? Why the ordinary man in the street? Is there any justice at all?

There seem to be three possible answers to this problem. The first is the simplest. "No, there is no justice. Heredity and the accident of environment account entirely for your condition at birth. No doubt, you can improve your situation to some extent, along the lines of your inherited capacities and with the help of a good education. But there is a limit. Shakespeare was very lucky. The idiot was extremely unfortunate."

The second answer is more or less as follows: "Certainly,

there is inequality, but there is justice also. Life is a handicap race. To whom much was given, from him much will be expected. Shakespeare had better be good. As for the idiot, as for the cripples and the poor, let them be patient. After this life, there will be another, a better existence, in which everything will be straightened out." This answer infuriates the socialist, who exclaims: "What hypocrisy! What religious opium! Clean up your slums, establish prenatal clinics, provide free education, share the profits of industry. Never mind your promise of justice in heaven. Let's have justice here on earth."

The third answer is the one given by Vedanta. It is more complex, but also more logical than the second, more optimistic than the first. "I quite agree," says the Vedantist, "that existence continues after death. I agree that our actions in this life will condition the circumstances of that existence; since the law of karma will not cease to operate. I don't know why you limit yourselves to two lives. I foresee thousands. Lives on this earth, and lives elsewhere. I believe that an accumulation of very good karma will cause the individual to be reborn in what may be described as 'heaven,' and that very bad karma will place him in a sort of 'hell.' Only, my heaven and my hell have a time limit, like life in the world. When the good or bad karma is exhausted, the individual will be reborn here on earth. I say this because I believe that human life has a peculiarity: it is the only condition in which one can create fresh karma. Elsewhere one merely enjoys or suffers the karmic effects of one's earthly actions.

"You claim that this particular birth was your beginning. I don't see why. Philosophically, your position is awkward, because it compels you to believe that the condition of the idiot and the genius of Shakespeare are due to the divine justice or injustice of some external power. God is supposed to bind one man and free another, and then tell them both to make the best of it. Why blame God? Why not say that the idiot is an idiot because of his past actions in previous lives? It may sound cruel, but it is much more consistent. Don't misunderstand me: I am not denying heredity. I believe that heredity operates. But I also believe that the sum of our karmas compels us to be born into a certain kind of family, under certain physical and economic conditions. You may ask: 'Who would choose to be an idiot?' I reply: 'Who would choose to be a dope addict?' Our thoughts and actions, apparently so casual and harmless, create these appalling tendencies; and the tendencies are finally too strong for us."

The Vedantist has finished, and we can begin to heckle him.

"If we had past lives, why can't we remember them?"

"Can you remember exactly what you did this time yesterday? Can you remember what it felt like to be sitting on your mother's lap at the age of eighteen months? As a matter of fact, there is a yoga technique of concentration which is supposed to enable you to recall your previous existences. I'm not asking you to believe this. You would have to try it for yourself; and it would be a stupid waste of time. If you want a working hypothesis which sounds scientific, can't you simply assume that we suffer a kind of amnesia? After all, birth must be a terrible shock."

"Your theory certainly removes the objection of divine injustice. But how do you account for the fact that karma ever started at all?"

"I can't. I only say, as I have said already, that the phenomenal universe is beginningless and endless; coexistent with the Reality. The law of karma was always in operation. It always will be."

"Then we just go up and down, getting better, getting worse, forever?"

"Certainly not. The individual can escape from karma at any given moment, as soon as he realizes that he is the Atman. Every individual will realize this, sooner or later. He must. The Atman within him will draw him to itself."

"And then?"

"When samadhi has been attained, the law of karma ceases to operate. No new karmas can be created. The liberated saint may live on in his human body, just as a wheel goes on revolving for a while after its motive power has stopped. But he will never be reborn, either in this world, or in any other karmic sphere."

"What's the difference between a man who has attained samadhi and an avatar?"

"The avatar has no past, no previous births as an individual. He has no karma at all. He enters the phenomenal universe and leaves it at will."

"What happens when everybody has attained samadhi? Won't the supply of individuals run out? Won't the universe cease to exist?"

"No. The ego-sense, which is the basis of individuality, will continue to work its way upward, through inanimate matter, through plant life, through the lower animals, into human form and consciousness. But how can we discuss these things? We stumble over our own words. The universe is an illusion. Our essential nature is Reality. We are never separated from it for an instant. The theory of karma is only valuable insofar as it reminds us of the extraordinary importance of our every thought and action, and of our responsibility toward each other. We have talked enough. Now do something. Start to practice yoga. Try to realize the Atman. All your questions will ultimately be answered, all your doubts will gradually disappear."

What Vedanta Means to Me

To suggest that I accepted Vedanta philosophy just because it convinced me intellectually would be to claim that I am a creature of pure reason. And, of course, I am nothing of the kind. We none of us are. The really decisive convictions of our lives are never arrived at through the power of arguments alone. The right teacher must appear at exactly the right moment in the right place; and his pupil must be in the right mood to accept what he teaches. But a description of the way in which these various factors combined, in my own case, to influence me, would be too long and complicated, and too frankly autobiographical, to fit the kind of article I am writing. All I can do here is to list some of the reasons why Vedanta appealed to me—reminding the reader, at the same time, that these reasons are only reasons; they really do not explain anything.

1. Vedanta is nondualistic. Psychologically, this was of the greatest importance to me; because of my fear and hatred of God as the father figure. I don't think I could ever have swallowed a philosophy that *began* with dualism. Vedanta began by telling me that I was the Atman, and that the Atman was Brahman; the God within was my own real nature, and the real nature of all that I experienced as to the external, surrounding universe. Having taught me this, it could go on to explain that this one immanent and transcendent Godhead may project all sorts of divine forms and incarnations which are, as the Gita says, its "million faces." To the eyes of this world, the One appears as many. Thus explained, dualism no longer seemed repulsive to me; for I could now think of the gods as mirrors in which man could dimly see what would otherwise be quite

invisible to him, the splendor of his own immortal image. By looking deeply and single-mindedly into these mirrors, you could come gradually to know your own real nature; and, when that nature, that Atman, was fully known and entered into, the mirror-gods would no longer be necessary, since the beholder would be absolutely united with his reflection. This approach to dualism via nondualism appealed so strongly to my temperament that I soon found myself taking part enthusiastically in the cult of Sri Ramakrishna, and even dropping into Christian churches I happened to be passing, to kneel for a while before the altar. Obviously, I had been longing to do this for years. I was a frustrated devotee.

2. Vedanta is not dogmatic. Previously, I had always thought of religion in terms of dogmas, commandments, and declarative statements. The teacher expounded the truth, the dogmatic ultimatum; you, the pupil, had only to accept it in its entirety. (Your sole alternative was to reject it altogether.) But Vedanta made me understand, for the first time, that a practical, working religion is experimental and empirical. You are always on your own, finding things out for yourself in your individual way. Vedanta starts you off with a single proposition, which is no more than a working hypothesis. "The Atman can be known. We say so, on the basis of the past experience of others. But we don't ask you to believe that. We don't want you to believe anything. All we ask is that you make a serious effort to get some spiritual experience for yourself, using the techniques of meditation which we shall teach you. If, after a reasonable period of time, you have found nothing, then never mind Ramakrishna, never mind Christ, never mind anybody; you are entitled to say boldly that our teaching is a lie, and we shall respect you for saying so. We have no use for blind believers." Who could decline such a challenge? "This," I said to myself, "is what religion is really all about. Religion isn't a course of passive indoctrination; it is an active search for awareness. Why didn't somebody ever tell me so before?" The question was, of

course, absurdly unfair. I had been "told" this innumerable times. Every moment of my conscious existence had contained within itself this riddle—"What is life for?"—and its answer: "To learn what life means." Every event, every encounter, every person and object I had met, had restated question and answer in some new way. Only, I hadn't been ready to listen. Now, as I came to learn something about practical mysticism, I was greatly astonished to find how closely the recorded experiences of Hindu and Christian (not to mention Buddhist and Taoist, Sufi and Jewish) mystics are interrelated. And thus another group of my anti-Christian prejudices was liquidated, along with my ignorance.

3. Vedanta does not emphasize the vileness of man's mortal nature or the enormity of sin. It dwells, rather, on the greatness of man's eternal nature and refuses to dignify sin by allowing it too much dramatic value. Vivekananda warns us not to think of ourselves as sinners; such seeming humility can easily degenerate into perverse masochism. We shall do better to remind ourselves continually of what is godlike in man and try to be worthy of that. As for our sins, we shall not atone for them by sentimental orgies of contrition. What we have to understand is simply this: every act has consequences, and we are paid for everything we think or say or do with an absolute, automatic fairness—neither too much nor too little. If we persist in performing acts which promote a strengthening of the ego-sense, then we shall find that we are becoming increasingly alienated from the knowledge of the Atman within us. And if we perform such acts, we have nobody but ourselves to blame. This is no romantic tragedy of doom; it is merely silly. For we can stop whenever we really want to and are ready to pray sincerely for strength, to the source of strength in our own minds.

This is the message of Vedanta as Vivekananda preaches it. Like many others before me, I heard it with an almost incredulous joy. Here, at last, was a man who believed in God and yet dared to condemn the indecent grovelings of the sin-obsessed Puritans I had so much despised in my youth. I loved him at once, for his bracing self-reliance, his humor, and his courage. He appealed to me as the perfect anti-Puritan hero: the enemy of Sunday religion, the destroyer of Sunday gloom, the shocker of prudes, the breaker of traditions, the outrager of conventions, the comedian who taught the deepest truths in idiotic jokes and frightful puns. That humor had its place in religion, that it could actually be a mode of spiritual self-expression, was a revelation to me; for, like every small boy of Puritan upbringing, I had always longed to laugh out loud and make improper noises in church. I didn't know, then, that humor has also had its exponents in the Christian tradition. I knew nothing, for example, about St. Philip Neri, who allowed children to play games around the altar during mass, and who would sit on the pope's lap and pull his beard in fun.

Speaking of Vivekananda brings me to mention three more or less incidental considerations which, nevertheless, played an important part in my acceptance of Vedanta. They may sound somewhat trivial to the intelligent reader. I must remind him that my attitude toward religion at that time was not only unintelligent but very naive.

First, I found Vedanta all the more reassuring because its latest great examplars—Ramakrishna himself, and Vivekananda, Brahmananda, and their brother disciples—had lived so recently. The figures of the major Christian saints, not to mention that of the historic Jesus of Nazareth, are all somewhat dimmed by the passage of time. But Ramakrishna died only eighteen years before I was born; I have met three people who knew Vivekananda; and Brahmananda was the guru of my own guru, Swami Prabhavananda. These are not remote inhabitants of another epoch, but still-living, vivid presences. Photographs of them exist. Records of their sayings and doings are detailed and reliable. You can easily imagine what it would have been like to encounter them as human beings. And, for this reason alone, the guarantee which their lives offer of the truth of

Vedanta is singularly impressive. Imagine what it would mean to a Christian to know so much about—let us say—St. Francis of Assisi!

Secondly, Vedanta—or rather, the Vedanta society of America—attracted me because it was a small movement, without great wealth or the slightest pretensions to political influence. My horror and contempt for the political maneuvers of the leading Christian churches was very strong at that time, and it has not lessened since. No amount of argument will ever convince me that interference in world diplomacy by religious bodies is anything but evil. If, at some future date, the Vedanta society becomes involved in American politics, then it will have betrayed Ramakrishna, just as the churches have, in this respect, betrayed Christ. "My kingdom is not of this world" is said, or implied, by all true spiritual prophets. Meanwhile, it is, at least, a hopeful indication of future policy that the Ramakrishna Order of India, which is certainly neither poor nor lacking in influence, refused to support Gandhi's noncooperation movement, despite its sympathy for his cause.

Thirdly, I liked Vedanta because it talked Sanskrit. By this I do not mean that I am a lover of the obscure and exotic; quite the reverse. But I was suffering, at the period of my first acquaintance with Vedanta, from a semantic block against the words which were associated with my Christian upbringing: God, savior, comforter, soul, heaven, redemption, love, salvation, etc., etc. To some of these, indeed, my reaction was so violent that I would wince and clench my fists whenever they were uttered. I could only approach the subject of mystical religion with the aid of a brand new vocabulary. Sanskrit supplied it. Here were a lot of new words, exact, antiseptic, uncontaminated by use in bishops' sermons, schoolmasters' lectures, politicians' speeches. To have gone back along the old tracks, to have picked up the old phrases and scraped them clean of their associations—that job would have been too disgusting for a beginner. But now it wasn't necessary. Every idea could be made over, restated in the new language. And restatement was what I most needed; as a mental discipline and even as an alibi, since it was embarrassing to admit to myself that I had been so intolerant. . . .

I have written all this; and yet I have really said nothing. I have failed to explain what Vedanta means to me. Perhaps that was inevitable. Religion, as I have already suggested, is not taught by one intelligence to another but caught through the influence of one personality upon another. And how is one to describe this process? I don't even begin to understand it, myself. I only know that, as far as I am concerned, the guru-disciple relationship is at the center of everything that religion means to me. It is the one reality of which I am never in doubt, the one guarantee that I shall ultimately surmount my own weakness and win through to knowledge of eternal strength, peace, and joy. Without this relationship, my life would be a nightmare of fear, boredom, and disgust. If, having known it, one could in some terrible way be deprived of it again, then that would be to experience hell, right here on earth. Personally, I do not worry about this, because I do not believe that the guru can ever abandon his disciples, either voluntarily or invo-luntarily. I believe that their relationship survives death, acci-dent, betrayal, and every other kind of hazard. No one, of course, can prove me wrong—or right. And I must admit that I have an exceedingly optimistic nature.

VEDANTA AND THE WEST

I wish to raise a fundamentally important question: "Has Vedanta philosophy a specific contribution to make to the religious thinking of the West?" Or, to put it in another way. "Is there already something that we can describe as Occidental, in contradistinction to Oriental, Vedanta?"

Vedanta is a nondualistic philosophy. It teaches that Brahman (the ultimate Reality behind the phenomenal universe) is "One without a second." Brahman is beyond all attributes. Brahman is not conscious; Brahman *is* consciousness. Brahman does not exist; Brahman *is* existence. Brahman is the Atman (the eternal Nature) of every human being, creature, and object. Vedanta teaches us that life has no other purpose than this— that we shall learn to know ourselves for what we really are; that we shall reject the superficial ego-personality which claims that "I am Mr. Smith; I am other than Mr. Brown," and know, instead, that "I am the Atman; Mr. Brown is the Atman; the Atman is Brahman; there is nothing anywhere but Brahman; all else is appearance, transience, and unreality."

Nevertheless—since philosophy was made for man, and not vice versa—the exponents of Vedanta have had to recognize that a strict and arduous discipline of intellectual discrimination between Brahman and non-Brahman, Real and unreal, is not for the average run of humanity. The unillumined mind is physically incapable of imagining Brahman; for it deals in pictures and words, and Brahman eludes all description. Therefore we turn naturally toward the highest that we can imagine—the God with attributes which are perfections of our own virtues, or the godlike man who has actually lived amongst us upon earth and can strengthen and purify us by his example.

These we worship and toward these we aspire, hoping, through our devotion, to become like them. Thus, cults are born.

Vedanta philosophy does not in any way condemn the cult. It only reminds the cultist that the cult is not an end in itself. The God or godlike man whom we worship must not be allowed to come between us and the knowledge that worshiped and worshiper are, essentially, both projections of the one Brahman. What we adore in a Christ, a Buddha, in Kali or Jehovah or Kwan-yin, is our own Atman, our eternal Nature. In these divine personalities, that Nature is revealed; in ourselves it is more or less obscured. Nevertheless they exist in order that we may know ourselves. And, in the ultimate light of union with Brahman, they are merged and vanish.

In India, therefore, Vedanta has endured through the ages as a nondualistic philosophical structure sustaining and inter-relating many cults of Gods and divine incarnations. Misunder-standing of this fact has led some Western critics to assume that India is polytheistic. She is not. What is mistaken for poly-theism is the recognition that "the Truth is one, but sages call it by various names," and that different partial aspects of Truth will appeal to various kinds of religious temperament. The alternative to this so-called "polytheism" is the cruel and ugly sectarianism which claims a monopoly of truth for its own particular cult and is usually ready to persecute in order to enforce that monopoly. Such monopolistic cultism is emphati-cally rejected by Vedanta.

When Swami Vivekananda first visited the United States he did not come as the missionary of a Ramakrishna cult but as an exponent of Vedanta philosophy. In the majority of his lectures, he referred to Ramakrishna very seldom or not at all. Later, back in India, when he talked about this period, he was accustomed to say: "If I had preached the personality of Sri Ramakrishna, I might have converted half the world; but that kind of conversion is short-lived. So instead I preached Ramak-rishna's principles. If people accept the principles they will eventually accept the personality."

In its work in the Western hemisphere and in Europe, the Ramakrishna Order has followed Vivekananda's wise and far-sighted policy. The swamis of the order, in their public lectures, stress the Vedantic principles of Ramakrishna rather than his personality; Ramakrishna is presented always as an exemplar (and not the *only* exemplar) of Vedanta; and much is said about the relation of Vedanta to the teachings of Christ and the Christian saints.

Naturally, each Vedanta center maintains a cult of Ramakrishna for those who wish to join in worshiping him. But this is a matter of individual choice, and no student of Vedanta need necessarily take part in this cult, much less discard his loyalty to any other divine personality. Indeed, the Vedantist must do homage to all the divine personalities, since all are expressions of the one truth of Brahman.

In the West, the cult of Ramakrishna is still in its infancy and therefore still surrounded by the external symbols of Hindu religion. There will always be those who are temperamentally drawn to these externals, who prefer Sanskrit to English chants, who like to wear saris and perform pujas according to the ancient Indian rituals. Nor is there anything undesirable in this; the rituals of Hinduism are very beautiful, and they help one to imagine Ramakrishna within his own cultural setting, to picture him amidst the actual circumstances of his life on earth. Nevertheless, such practices are not for everybody; and Ramakrishna certainly never intended that all his Western followers should be turned into synthetic Hindus. Just as Jesus, through the ages, has lost much of his specifically Jewish character, so the figure of Ramakrishna will gradually become less and less specifically Indian. It cannot and should not be otherwise.

The cult of Ramakrishna may well grow to worldwide proportions, but it will never, unless his teaching is utterly betrayed, become an exclusive cult. Such a cult would be Ramakrishna without Vedanta; a denial of its founder. For Ramakrishna's gift to the West is the Vedanta philosophy which he restated and practically demonstrated in his own life. And it is Vedanta, rather than the special cult of Ramakrishna, which promises to exert a growing influence upon our Western thought in the immediate future.

At this point it is perhaps advisable to remark that a knowledge of Vedanta did not, of course, enter the Western world for the first time in 1893, with Swami Vivekananda. Schopenhauer; Emerson, Thoreau, and their circle; Max Mueller and his fellow orientalists—to name only a few of the swami's many forerunners—had all studied, discussed, and publicized the philosophy long before that date. What Vivekananda *did* bring to the West was the living example of a man wholly dedicated to the practice of Vedanta—an example infinitely more inspiring and convincing than any book, as Emerson himself would have been the first to admit.

Again, it must be understood that the Ramakrishna Order has never claimed to be the sole authentic source of Vedantic teaching in the West. Such a claim would be absurd. Obviously, there must be many reliable individual teachers to be found in different parts of the Americas and Europe. Such teachers, when met, may be tested very simply. One need only ask them: "What is the aim of your teaching?" If the answer is: "To show you how to know your real Nature; how to become united with Brahman," then the teacher is a true Vedantist. If the answer is: "To show you how to obtain power over others, how to become rich, how to become strong and beautiful and healthy, how to prolong your life, how to read the future, how to summon spirits to do your will," then he is not. This statement may sound ridiculously self-evident, but it is worth making at the present time, when spiritualism, astrology, clairvoyance, mental healing, and the study of occult symbolism preoccupy hundreds of thousands of people. Such studies are often founded upon ancient Hindu lore—the practice of astrology, for example, is still very popular in India—and they tend to be surrounded by an atmosphere of "oriental mystery." But they have nothing whatever to do with the aims of Vedanta.

And now—to return to our main topic—in what manner is the influence of Vedanta most likely to make itself felt?

As far as organized Christianity is concerned, Vedanta would seem to have very little chance of a hearing. The cult of Christ, as preached by the Catholic and Protestant churches, is an exclusive cult. It cannot admit the Vedantist's acceptance of other divine incarnations; and it must find his homage to Christ inadequate, since this is not an exclusive homage. And there are other, even more serious grounds for disagreement. For Vedanta also teaches the practice of mysticism; it claims, that is to say, that man may directly know and be united with his eternal Nature, the Atman, through meditation and spiritual discipline, without the aid of any church or delegated minister. Organized Christianity has long since condemned this idea as Gnosticism and has been inclined to question the insights of the mystic, even when he or she has remained an obedient member of the congregation. It cannot be denied that Vedanta does challenge the Church's claim to central importance as the body of Christ upon earth. It does exalt the validity of the mystic's direct experience far above the authority of creeds, dogmas, and scriptures. And its attitude to the problem of sin is, from the orthodox Christian standpoint, both incorrect and subversive.

I can see only one little door through which Vedanta might squeeze into Christendom, and that is the Society of Friends. The Quaker doctrine of the inward light is in general agreement with the principles of Vedanta. For the rest, there will be many broad-minded individuals within the churches who will find the study of Vedanta helpful and who will manage to reconcile at least some part of its teaching with their own traditional beliefs. More than this one can hardly hope for, failing a revolutionary reversal of policy by Christian religious leaders.

When, however, we consider the sciences, the prospects of Vedanta are much more encouraging. It is now generally, if rather vaguely, admitted that the trend of scientific thinking is away from materialistic atheism and toward an hypothesis which does not exclude the concept of a transcendent consciousness. If this is granted, we may claim with some assurance that Vedanta philosophy is superior to Christian theology as a potential bridge between science and religion. It is a striking fact—already remarked on by several outstanding scientists—that the world picture presented by Vedanta is largely in accord with the latest theories of astronomy and atomic physics. Vedantic influences are also becoming apparent in the field of psychology—as, for instance, in the recent work of Jung.

I believe, then, that Vedanta is most likely to influence the West through the medium of scientific thought. In this terrible epoch, when our power to do harm seems at length adequate to the evil of our intentions, we are accustomed to blame science for putting the weapons into our hands. Yet science, like the Hindu goddess Kali, is above good and evil; impartially, she gives us whatever we ask for, and her gifts may prove to be curses or blessings. At our bidding, the men of science have discovered the secret of atomic energy. Can they also discover, before it is too late, a moral sanction which will curb the power of the atom and direct it to peaceful and productive uses? Can science find us a new philosophical synthesis, a restatement of the eternal truths in terms which our modern agnosticism is able to accept?

That is a question which only the future can answer. Meanwhile, an unprecedented exchange of ideas is going on between East and West. We are giving the East our technology and our philosophy of dialectical materialism. What are we getting in return? If it is a greater understanding of what India and ancient China have to teach us, combined with a rediscovery of our own neglected spiritual potentialities—in fact, an Occidental Vedanta—then we certainly have the best of the bargain.

HYPOTHESIS AND BELIEF

If a member of the so-called intellectual class joins any religious group or openly subscribes to its teaching, he will have to prepare himself for a good deal of criticism from his unconverted and more skeptical friends. Some of these may be sympathetic and genuinely interested; others will be covertly satirical, suspicious, or quite frankly hostile and dismayed. It will be suggested to the convert, with a greater or lesser degree of politeness, that he has "sold out," betrayed the cause of Reason, retreated in cowardice from "the realities of life," and so forth. Henceforward, his conduct will be narrowly watched for symptoms of pretentiousness, priggishness, prudery, and all other forms of puritanism. Certain topics will either be altogether avoided in his presence, or they will be presented in the form of a challenge, to see how he will take them.

The convert himself, self-conscious and badly rattled, is almost sure to behave unnaturally. Either he will preach at his old friends and bore them, thus confirming their worst suspicions. Or he will make desperate efforts to reassure them, by his manner and conversation, that he is still "one of the gang." He will be the first to blaspheme, the first to touch upon the delicate subject. And his friends, far from feeling relieved, will be sincerely shocked.

One question, especially, he must learn to expect. It will be asked by the most candid, by those who really want to know: "Yes, of course, I can quite understand why you did it, in a way . . . but tell me, do you actually *believe* all that?" This question is particularly distressing to the convert, because, if he is to be honest, he will have to answer: "No. I don't—yet."

The "all that" to which the questioner refers will vary in detail and mode of formulation, according to the religious group the convert happens to have chosen. In essence, however, it can always be described by what Aldous Huxley has called "the minimum working hypothesis." This word *hypothesis* is extremely significant, but it will probably be overlooked by the outside observer, who prefers to simplify his picture of the world's religions by regarding their teachings as "creeds" and "dogmas." Nevertheless, a statement of religious doctrine can be properly called a creed only by those who know it to be true. It remains an hypothesis as long as you are not quite sure. Spiritual truth is, by definition, directly revealed and experienced: it cannot be known at second hand. What is revealed truth to a Christ is merely hypothetical truth to the vast majority of his followers; but this need not prevent the followers from trusting in Christ's personal integrity and in the authenticity of his revelation, *as far as Christ himself is concerned*. One can feel sure that Einstein is neither a fraud nor a lunatic, and that he has actually discovered the law of relativity; and still fail, in a certain sense, to "believe" in the conception of space-time, just because one has not yet personally understood it.

There is, even nowadays, a good deal of loose and unrealistic talk about "the conflict between religion and science." I call this kind of talk unrealistic because it suggests that "science," and hence scientists, are one hundred percent materialistic; and that "religion" is based upon the blind, hundred percent acceptance of dogmas which are incapable of scientific proof. Modern science is, of course, very far from being materialistic. In the nineteenth century, it is true, science did pass through a phase of mechanistic materialism. But the scientist himself never has been, and never could be, an absolute materialist. The scientist is a human being. The absolute materialist, if he existed, would have to be some sort of nonhuman creature, completely lacking the human faculty of intuition, a mere machine for measuring and making calculations. If a human being could become a truly convinced materialist, he would never have the heroism to get up in the morning, shave, and eat his breakfast. His world picture would be too terrible for even the boldest heart to contemplate; and, within twenty-four hours, he would have committed suicide.

Similarly, a religion based upon blind faith could not possibly survive, as all the world religious have survived, for hundreds and thousands of years. Religion lives, and is revived, from age to age, because of the direct revelation of the few, the saints, who win for themselves a personal knowledge of spiritual reality. Religion survives *in spite of* blind faith, priestly persecution, ecclesiastical politics; in spite of superstition and ignorance amongst the masses of its adherents. Most of us cannot understand this, because our imagination refuses to grasp the gigantic influence and importance of the saint as a historical phenomenon. Whereas the persecution and the ignorance stand out brutally from the pages of history in red and black, plain for all to see. Nine times out of ten, when we use the word *religion,* we are really referring to the crimes or follies committed in religion's name.

There is no conflict between true religion and true science, but there is a great deal of bickering between religious dogmatists and scientific pedants. The dogmatist states his case, or rather, presents his dogmatic ultimatum. The scientifically trained pedant reminds him, none too patiently, that his assertions cannot be verified by the microscope, the slide rule, or the laboratory experiment. Therefore, he continues, quite rightly, the dogma is merely another hypothesis. And, he will probably add that hypotheses which are incapable of scientific proof do not interest him, anyway. At this point, a deadlock is reached, and the two men part in mutual annoyance.

But now let us suppose that, instead of the tiresome, dogmatic convert (who is unconvincing because he has not personally experienced the truth of what he asserts) Christ himself should enter the scientist's laboratory, and make the very same statements which the convert makes. How would the scientist react? If the scientist were a pure, nonhuman materialist, he would, of course, remain completely unconvinced. But, since he is a creature of emotion and intuition as well as of reason, the chances are that he would be impressed, not rationally but emotionally, by the personality of Christ and the tremendous psychological impact of such a meeting. In spite of his scientific training, he would venture to trust his intuition. He would say to himself: "Although my scientific methods of analysis cannot deal with these statements, my intuition tells me that this man has some authority for his words."

This raises the question of what we may call "the credibility of the witness." The jury in a court of law does not, or should not, judge a case entirely by scientific (i.e., rational) method: it relies, also, on intuition. It decides to believe a witness or not to believe him—sometimes in defiance of considerable circumstantial evidence. There is, also, the factor of corroboration. If two or more witnesses support each other, and make an impression of being truthful, the case is apt to turn in their favor.

When we begin to examine the assertions of the great religious teachers, we shall have to behave like jurymen. Reason can help us, no doubt, and it must be brought to bear on the case; but reason will not take us all the way. It can only deliver a provisional verdict. It can only say: "This is possible," or "Perhaps . . ." Next, we must ask ourselves: "What sort of men are telling us this? Are they charlatans? Do they seem sane? Do their lives bear out the truth of what they preach?" And, again: "Do they, substantially, agree with each other's testimony?" On this second point, however, there can be little argument. The basis of essential agreement between the great religious teachers of the world is very firm and can easily be demonstrated by documentary evidence. Any student of comparative religion can reconstruct "the minimum working hypothesis." Nevertheless, it is quite possible to decide that Buddha, Christ, Shankara, St. Francis, and Ramakrishna were all mad, or self-deluded, and therefore not to be taken seriously. If that is the verdict, then our inquiry ends.

But, if the world's teachers were not mad, then, as all must agree, their teaching has universal application and implies an obligation to put it into practice, in our own lives. And so we are faced by the next question: "Am I dissatisfied with my life as it is at present? And, if so, am I sufficiently dissatisfied to want to do anything about it?"

Here the majority and the minority definitely part company. Buddha said that human life is miserable, but he did not say that everybody thinks it is. Not all the socially underprivileged are dissatisfied, as every reformer knows, to his despair. And this is even truer of spiritual poverty than of economic lack. Life contains a number of vivid sense pleasures, and the gaps of despondency and boredom between them can be filled more or less adequately by hard work, sleep, the movies, drink, and daydreaming. Old age brings lethargy, and morphia will help you at the end. Life is not so bad, if you have plenty of luck, a good physique, and not too much imagination. The disciplines proposed by the spiritual teachers are drastic, and the lazy will shrink back from them. They are tedious, also, and this will discourage the impatient. Their immediate results are not showy, and this will deter the ambitious. Their practice is apt to make you appear ridiculous to your neighbors. Vanity, sloth, and desire will all intervene to prevent a man from setting his foot upon the path of religious effort.

Disregarding all these obstacles, and they are tremendous, the beginner will have to say to himself: "Well, I am going to try. I believe that my teacher is sane and honest. I don't believe in his teachings with the whole of my mind, and I won't pretend that I do, but I have enough belief to make a start. My reason is not offended. My approach is strictly experimental. I will put myself into his hands and trust him at least as far as I would trust my doctor. I will try to live the kind of life which he prescribes. If, at the end of three or four years, I can conscientiously say that I have done what was asked of me and had no results whatsoever, then I will give up the whole attempt as a bad job."

ON THE LOVE OF GOD

Narada* tells us that "the path of devotion is the easiest path to attain God."

"The path of devotion," called *bhakti yoga* in Sanskrit, is the approach to God through love. The *bhakta* makes a continual conscious effort to love God and to feel God's love for him. To this end, he repeats God's name and performs ritual worship. In order to have a particular object for his worship, he fixes his mind upon one chosen aspect of God or one out of the several divine incarnations. Narada, like the other great teachers, assures us however that as the bhakta's devotion grows, he will become more and more aware that he is actually worshiping the God within himself which is his own true nature. In the supreme state of bhakti, worshiper and worshiped will be realized as one.

As defined by Hindu philosophy, there are four ways of attaining this unitive knowledge of God: *bhakti yoga, karma yoga, jnana yoga,* and *raja yoga.* Karma yoga is the approach to God through selfless action—action performed without desire for personal gain or fear of unpleasant consequences; it is often practiced by serving God through one's fellowmen. Jnana yoga is the approach through discrimination between the real and the unreal; when all transitory phenomena have been rigorously analyzed and rejected, God alone remains and becomes known by a process of elimination. Raja yoga is the approach through intensive practice of meditation.

Now it is obvious that three of these yogas demand qualities and powers which are not possessed by everyone or even by a

*A great saint of Indian lore.

large majority of human beings. Karma yoga calls for heroic energy as well as great humility and patience; jnana yoga for an exceptionally acute intellect; raja yoga for unwavering concentration and control of the senses. Compared with them, the practice of bhakti yoga appears far simpler, less austere, and more inviting. Besides, while we may not flatter ourselves that we have exceptional energy, intellect, or concentration, we are all firmly convinced that we are capable of love. Therefore we readily accept Narada's statement—that bhakti is the easiest of the yogas.

Too readily, in most cases. For do most of us realize what it is that we are accepting? Have we any idea at all what Narada means by loving God? Have we ever fully considered what we ourselves mean when we use, or misuse, the word *love*? Have we, indeed, ever truly loved anybody?

There is a phrase which was once current in everyday conversation and popular with songwriters: "to be in love with love." When grown-ups were talking about the emotions of their teenage children they would say, with indulgent smiles, "Oh, she's just in love with love, that's all it is"—meaning that the teenager in question wasn't really in love but only indulging in romantic self-deception. *Real* love, the grown-ups implied, was something the teenagers would learn later, something adult and serious and down to earth—and there was a hint of grim satisfaction in their tone, as when combat veterans allude to what awaits a raw recruit.

The phrase has gone out of fashion, but the attitude persists; real love is still defined in terms of the consequences and responsibilities it creates—social acceptance or disgrace, marriage or divorce, wealth or debts, childbearing or childlessness, domestic slavery or desertion. When people seem to be talking about love they are in fact discussing its consequences, more often than not. Indeed it is sometimes hard to see the love for the consequences. The relationship usually discussed is, of course, the sexual relationship. But no one can deny that the relations between parents and children, friends, colleagues, even animals and their owners, can become equally strained in times of crisis and create similar economic and social difficulties, similar torments of jealousy and merciless struggles of opposing egos.

There are many people, certainly, who manage to loosen the bonds of their own egotism enough to be able to love each other more or less unselfishly throughout their lives. Love, or at any rate the memory of love, is always present to some degree even in the unhappiest of relationships. And, as Narada reminds us, all love—no matter how the ego may distort or restrict it— is in essence divine. But the question remains, can a consideration of these states of imperfect human love be of any help to us in understanding the concept of bhakti yoga?

The love of God described by Narada is a love in which there can be no jealousy, no struggle of egos, no desire for material advantage or exclusive possession, no dread of desertion; a love which is incapable of unhappiness. Even the pain of temporary alienation from God cannot be called unhappy; for the devotee who feels it knows, simply because he does feel it, that God exists and that the relationship between them is live and real.

But this concept of a love without unhappiness is just what we, as beginners in the study of bhakti, can scarcely grasp. That isn't love at all, we say to ourselves; it's cold, unnatural, inhuman. For we must admit, if we are frank, that we have become so conditioned by the world's view of love that we actually need to be made jealous, need to suffer craving and anxiety, need to make the hopeless demand for exclusive possession—because, without those familiar pains, we are unable to enjoy the respites from pain which we call happiness in love.

So perhaps there is still some usefulness in the old silly sounding phrase; to be in love with love. Perhaps it can be helpful in giving us our first glimpse of what is meant by bhakti. Let us stop thinking of love as a relationship between two individual egos and concentrate on the capacity for love which is within each one of us. It may be very small but it is our own and it cannot fail us. We can all agree that our love, when it is thus regarded without relation to any external object, is both lovable for itself and completely free from desire or pain. And in this way we can begin to grasp the idea that love is God.

RELIGION WITHOUT PRAYERS

In the April 1946 issue of *Commentary,* Professor Irwin Edman has written an article called *Religion without Tears.* It asks the question "Do moderns need an otherworldly faith?" and its answer is, "No, they don't."

This article is worth discussing from a Vedantist point of view, not only because it is moderately and intelligently written, without undue aggressiveness, but because it represents a large body of opinion in the world today.

Professor Edman begins by noting that many people are now turning to religion because they despair of conditions in our society. The nineteenth century believed that scientific progress would automatically increase human happiness; instead, it has brought us to the use of the atomic bomb.

If anything, of late the dissatisfaction with pure mechanism and pure materialism has grown even more acute. In a society increasingly dominated by things and threatened by them, an account of the universe seems a poor thing which leaves out, or seems to leave out, what human beings chiefly value—the intimations of truth, goodness, and beauty in their lives. The saints and the prophets still seem to say more that is relevant to human personality, to its hopes, its aims, its aspirations than do the bleak formulas of the mechanists and the behaviorists. . . .

If the world of science remains alien to our inmost spiritual needs, where shall we turn? Well, in this age as in previous ones, those who are disillusioned by the formulas and disinherited by the symbols and traditions of the religious past, turn in whatever direction they see a gleam of meaning, hope or consolation. Intellectuals are repeatedly discovering that though they may think they have outgrown theology, they are still in need of religion, of—in the old yet still pregnant phrase—a faith by which to live . . . The dilemma is intellectual, and this explains, I think, why solutions are frequently sought by a revolt against intellectualism altogether . . . The new cults of mysticism at least give surcease from thinking; they provide or seem to provide sesames to protoplasmic peace.

Other escapes are sought in less obviously non-intellectual ways, but anti-rational ones none the less. There is the cult itself, the reassertion of the basic importance of ritual in religion. The sharing of a common ceremonial hallowed by tradition removes one of the curses of the modern world, the sense of belonging nowhere, of having no bonds or attachments, of being a bleak anonymity in a vast megalopolis. Even the retreat to dogma is often an unintellectual or even an anti-intellectual one. It is a flight to authority; it obviates the necessity of coming to one's own even bleak conclusions . . . There is no doubt that mysticism, ritual and dogma have been assuagements for many persons of a sense of insecurity, of loneliness and emptiness in the modern world . . .

What does Professor Edman really mean by these remarks? He means, as far as I can understand him, that mysticism *can* degenerate into vague, irresponsible sentimentality, that ritual *may* be practiced as an empty, formal observance, that dogma *is often* only a crutch for weak and lazy minds. Very true. The same thing might be said of one's attitude to a Shakespeare sonnet, a Fourth of July parade, or the Bill of Rights. I have known people who were extremely vague, sentimental, and dogmatic when discussing the theory of democracy or the Marxian dialectic.

Religion, certainly, is what we make of it. Our effort is its reward. Has Professor Edman read Shankara or Vivekananda? I am sure he has. Then how can he possibly write that mysticism offers us "surcease from thinking"? What greater demands could be made upon the human brain than Shankara makes— this merciless, unwearying process of discrimination which he asks us to apply to every moment of our lives? What greater intellectual independence is there than Vivekananda's, who would not even accept the teaching of his own beloved master until he had tested it for himself? Mysticism is empirical, or it is nothing. Ritual is a personal act of recollection and self-dedication, or it is meaningless. Dogmas are hypothetically accepted truths, or they are silly.

Is mysticism otherworldly? Not in Professor Edman's sense. The I.W.W. used to sing:

> You'll get pie
> In the sky
> When you die—
> It's a lie.

And they were right. It is the most pernicious of all lies— the real "opium of the people." No great spiritual teacher has ever uttered it. Vedanta, with its doctrine of karma and reincarnation, teaches the exact opposite: every thought, every word, and every action will be paid for, in this life or in lives to come. Believe, if you wish, that death is the end. But do not dare to imagine that you can get away with murder, and be rewarded for it with "pie," into the bargain. If there *is* a personal survival, it follows, surely, that our problems, our karmas, will survive with us, and that these karmas will determine the conditions of our future existence.

However, that is not the point. What has to be emphasized, again and again, is that mystical religion does not lay nearly so much stress on the question of personal survival as its critics seem to imagine. Buddha did not promise his disciples an otherworldly heaven; he promised the "ending of sorrow," here and now. The mystics offer us a way of happiness here in this world; they offer us a way of understanding the true nature of this present life. Certainly, the basis of this happiness and understanding is outside time and circumstance—it is within this world but not *of* it. In that sense, alone, it is "otherworldly."

Professor Edman continues:

The first rehabilitation necessary is a revival of faith in man's own potentialities and in man's own hopes. The lack of confidence in these lies in the fact that by a century-old diffidence men have not trusted their own ideals unless they came from a world beyond this world. But when it is realized, as Lucretius long ago realized, that the most generous and flowering of human values are growths of these same natural energies out of which plants and animals grow, a wonderful resurgence both of human hope and of cosmic piety is possible . . . The first step needed in the rehabilitation of the human faith in candidly human values is a rediscovery of the reach and scope of human nature itself.

Professor Edman deplores the fact that "there has long been bred in the human imagination a distrust of anything tainted with the material, the fleshly, the earthly." Did the mystics, in fact, feel this distrust? Christ would not condemn the woman taken in adultery; Ramakrishna liked to talk to drunkards and once offered consecrated food to a cat; St. Francis preached to the birds; Vivekananda wrote, "See no difference between ant and angel; every worm is brother to the Nazarene." I suppose Professor Edman would object that Ramakrishna was not worshiping the cat *as* a cat, but as Eternal Reality within the creature. He is quite right, but where does this lead him? He says he wants to discover the reach and scope of human nature itself. Doesn't human nature include the mystical experience of Eternal Reality? Aren't saints human beings? How are we to have faith in some of man's own potentialities while we reject others? I do not want to sound captious, but I simply cannot follow Professor Edman here. He says,

Even theological ideas may be transcriptions of facts encountered and truths discovered in actual experience and in the natural world. Filial piety is a familiar human emotion. It becomes sanctified by a commandment, but the commandment simply dignifies what human beings deeply feel.

If "actual experience" is our criterion, can we honestly deny the experiences of spiritual religion? They, also, are deeply felt. And the world's scriptures simply dignify them.

But perhaps this is only playing with words. The end of the article, at any rate, is perfectly clear. It raises a very important question.

What is needed is not a counsel of escape into an emptiness called Nirvana or the Absolute. Rather the challenge is to an ordering of personal life through intelligent understanding so that the varied riches of human values may blend and fuse into a rich and vital happiness. And the challenge, too, is the making of a social order in which individuals may come to diversified felicities.

Individual lives cannot be ordered except in an ordered society. There cannot be healthy souls in a sick commonwealth. Thus, the central challenge to a naturalistic philosophy is that of a society harmonized through intelligence . . . The mystical sense that once declared us all the children of God can now find realization in the awareness of our common humanity. The sadness that comes from the recognition that individual life ends with the grave is mitigated for any generous mind by the continuity of the adventure of mankind, and the participation, even if briefly, in the shape of things to come.

This, of course, is the official philosophy of the Soviet Union. You work for the future, a willing cog in a great machine. You function for a while, wear out, and are discarded. It doesn't matter. The machine goes on.

As Professor Edman tacitly admits, it is a nonrational philosophy—that is to say, it demands faith. You must believe that the spiral of human progress really *is* ascending, that life on this earth will get better and better. It is a faith which is anchored in time, in the future. Only history can prove it right or wrong. Suppose the human species dies out? Suppose we blow ourselves up or hit a star? Then all our endeavors, *from a historical point of view,* will have been in vain.

Professor Edman would reply that we mustn't look on the dark side of things. We must have courage. Certainly we must—but where is this courage to be found? Only, it seems to me, in the doctrine of nonattached action, of work performed as ritual, which the *Bhagavad-Gita* teaches. Nonattached action, however, is a mystical idea—and so Professor Edman is forced to reject it.

If you reject mystical religion and, at the same time, lose your faith in an earthly utopia—what remains? Nothing but sheer stoicism; the grimmest and most heroic of man's philosophies. It is, indeed, a philosophy for heroes. Ordinary people will always shrink from it. I shrink from it myself. If this is all life offers, why should I stay alive?

My duty to society? What does this actually mean? On the level of "candidly human values," it means my neighbors, Smith, Jones, Robinson, and Brown. I quite like Smith, Jones bores me, Robinson I scarcely know, Brown I detest. If I am to work for them, to dedicate my life to them, I have somehow got to love them all. But how?

I can only love Smith, Jones, Robinson, and Brown—and two billion others—if I can see them *sub specie aeternitatis;* if I can learn to recognize, within each individual, the same Eternal Reality. In order to do this, I must first find the Eternal Reality within myself. You can't recognize what you don't know.

The search for Reality is a mystical search. It involves prayer and meditation and self-discipline—or, as Professor Edman would say, "religion with tears." Without it, I firmly believe, there can be no enduring cooperation between human beings. Without it, you cannot build the just city, on earth or anywhere else. The bricks simply will not hold together.

And yet I cannot help feeling, as I read this article—and many similar articles and books—that the humanistic materialists and the followers of mystical religion are not nearly so far apart as they imagine. Surely, with goodwill and effort on both sides, we can come to understand each other? Surely we can find a basis of agreement? We all want the same thing—a faith to live by. The need was never more urgent. We should study each other's ideas, not in a spirit of contemptuous criticism, but quietly and thoughtfully. If words and phrases, too long contaminated by hypocrisy and careless misuse, are getting between us, then we must reject them. The alternative is growing suspicion, the closing of minds, the hardening of hearts—and, ultimately, perhaps, persecution. And that, as we ought to have learned by this time, will help nobody.

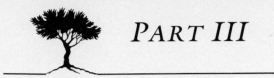

PART III

MY TEACHERS

WHO IS RAMAKRISHNA?

I once met a lady in Paris who as soon as we were introduced asked me to draw a picture of a horse—which I did, somewhat mystified. She then explained that she asked everybody she met to do this because it was amazing the different ways in which people draw pictures of horses. Some people only draw the head, some the whole body. Some draw the horse in one position, some in another. She had worked out a system by which she could judge people by knowing what kind of a horse or portion of a horse they would draw.

So, I was telling this to another of my friends and she said, "Oh, I think it is entirely too complicated, drawing horses. What *I* do is, I ask people, 'Who are you?' " She said, "You would be astounded, the different ways in which this question is answered. One person says, 'I am John Smith of Sycamore Road, Santa Monica.' Another says, 'I am a pharmacist's mate on such and such a ship.' Another says, 'I'm a screenwriter.' Another says, 'I'm Elvis Presley's maternal grandmother.' And then there are a few people who answer: '*Who am I?* My goodness, if I knew *that* I would know everything!' "

You will see the connection between this and the title "Who Is Ramakrishna?"

Now it's easy for me to tell you what many of you already know well—who Ramakrishna *was*. That is to say, who he was as a historical character. But, to engage to say who Ramakrishna *is*, what the full significance of this individual is, that is something which few people could attempt. Perhaps nobody could adequately express it in words. However, before we go on to these questions, I'm going to say a little bit in general about the background of Sri Ramakrishna.

The first thing is that the position of a holy man in India and the whole Indian approach to religion is a little different from what we have in the West. You see, in India what is considered basic is the religious experience of an individual—what he finds out for himself. In the West, we live of course in the tradition of Christianity, and we are used to thinking that the source of knowledge is ultimately in the Church, and that the Church defines spiritual experience, and that our spiritual experience is to be found within the Church, not as outsiders, not as individuals seeking for ourselves. In the West, we think of religion as the cult of Jesus Christ; that is to say, we cannot think of Christianity aside from the worship of this divine figure. But in India, one has to remember that there are a whole number of divine figures who may be the object of a cult of worship. You may worship one rather than another, choosing Krishna, let us say, for your Ideal and worshiping him in preference to, let us say, Kali the Mother of the Universe. And therefore in India it is much easier to understand that there are in fact two aspects to religion—worship, devotion to a divine figure, and the general philosophical approach to religion. Because, after all, what is religion? It begins at any rate with the question "What am I? What is there inside of me, if anything, other than my little personal ego which I know?"

In order to contact this other thing, this mystery which we sense to be not only within us but all around us in the universe, we may, and probably shall, approach it through the path of devotion. We say to ourselves, I am apparently not godlike. Therefore in order to find out if there *is* anything godlike in myself I will look toward somebody who is evidently godlike, and so I worship a Christ, or any other divine figure, and thus ennoble myself by dwelling upon what is evidently godlike in somebody outside of myself. But this, of course, although it is the approach for most of us, and perhaps the best, safest, and easiest approach, is still not the only approach. One must remember that there are people whose temperament shuns the idea of devotion as being too emotional, and who prefer an approach of intellectual discrimination—of trying to find out what is eternal by rejecting what is temporal and phenomenal. It is sometimes said that the path of discrimination is the path of saying "not this, not this," as we throw aside, one after another, all of the things in life which are not eternal, trying to see what it is that finally remains. And in the same way it is said that the path of devotion is saying "this, this," because everywhere we try to see the presence of God around us. Of course, in saying all of this I am taking a big jump, because the question that first arises is, not *how* do we seek God, but *why* should we seek God? Is there any necessity to do so? Is there any compulsion? Should one perhaps lead one's life on the surface of appearances and rely on a shot of morphia or good luck to finish you off without too much unpleasantness at the end?

The Hindus have no hesitation in answering this question, because they believe in reincarnation. It's important to bear this in mind when discussing the thought processes of a Hindu, because this is something that absolutely follows as a matter of course. They do not believe that death is the end. Therefore just getting through this life somehow or other is no good whatsoever, because you will be reborn and confronted with all the same unsolved problems and unfinished business to take care of again under, probably, less agreeable circumstances.

What the Hindus believe is that we are driven by our desires and compulsions to be born again and again, and they believe that liberation consists in freeing ourselves from the fetters of this desire, this compulsion, and so, as they put it, getting off the wheel of rebirth. They believe, therefore, that there is in fact a very definite reason why one should seek to know God, because in knowing God one comes to know one's own true nature, and in getting to know one's own true nature one realizes that one is not John Smith or Mary Brown, but that one is the Eternal. In knowing this, the bonds of desire are loosed, because one no longer wishes to be reborn in this cycle of individual lives, and one is freed and becomes a part of, so to speak, what one always was; that is to say, the Eternal.

So, the aim of religion in India is absolutely apparent. It is to obtain liberation through knowledge of God. And the way in which God is known is by meditating upon him, rendering service to him, which means, of course, rendering service to our fellow human beings and making it a kind of sacramental act, so that although you are working, let us say, in a hospital, you are really rendering the service to God. This distinction is important because if you try to render service only to individuals *as* individuals, you will find yourself minding very much if they aren't grateful to you, or if they misunderstand your intention, or if they don't sufficiently reward you for your services. But if you can render the service in a dispassionate manner, then this problem simply doesn't arise, because God is never ungrateful, he never fails to be present, he never in any way disappoints you, since you are offering your service to him. In India these various ways in which to know God are called "yogas." There is the yoga of service, the yoga of meditation, and the yoga of discrimination of which I was speaking awhile ago—the discrimination of trying to see always the real, and to separate the real from the unreal.

Now, of course, the practical test by which you know if somebody is really acquiring knowledge of God, is the test of character. Is this person's character being transformed? Is something happening to him? If a person is simply deluding himself, or autohypnotizing himself, then, of course, his character is not in the least bit transformed, he remains exactly as he was, and what is more, he doesn't acquire the power of projecting any kind of reassurance, any kind of spiritual force from himself, which you find in the case of all genuinely spiritual people. The whole atmosphere which they bring with them is in itself conducive to belief.

One of the simplest and most fundamental ways in which God is served in India is by means of the mantram, and this is a very important thing to know about, especially in connection with Sri Ramakrishna. When you are initiated by your teacher, he gives you a form of words, of sacred words which you are to repeat as often as possible and on all occasions, either aloud, or if you are among people, to yourself. This is called a mantra. At first sight this seems too idiotic even to discuss—that mumbling a lot of words, especially where in our case they are in a foreign language, could possibly do any good to anybody. However, the people who make money by advertising wouldn't laugh at such an idea. They know only too well that the mumbling of some equally silly sounding words will end up in your buying a certain breakfast product of theirs, and of course it is true that we are continually repeating mantras in our minds about our resentments, we are repeating the names of diseases that we fear we have, we are muttering about the Russians, and the Russians are muttering about us. So, after all, is this concept so silly, that by repeating the name of God, you can also produce an effect upon yourself? This is, I hope, for most of you a purely rhetorical question, because of course anybody who has used a mantra knows perfectly well that it makes a most tremendous impression upon the mind, and that it is in fact perhaps the one rope to which we can all hold firm throughout our day and throughout our lives.

There is only one other thing that I want to touch on before speaking of Ramakrishna himself, and that is something to which it is necessary to refer, but which for most of us seems so strange that it has no relation to our everyday experience whatsoever. That is, the state of samadhi. The result of prolonged meditation is, of course, that the mind becomes more and more indrawn and concentrated upon its object. And when this process has become very far advanced, a phenomenon takes place which is called, in Sanskrit, samadhi, which is a state of identification in which the meditator becomes one with the thing upon which he is meditating. The mind is so completely indrawn that the body itself shows no signs of life, and all outer consciousness is lost, and yet a person in the state of samadhi is not unconscious. He is tremendously, powerfully, conscious on another plane, and becomes aware of his identity with the object upon which he is meditating. In other words, if you are meditating upon God you become aware of that in your nature which is divine. This is a kind of paradox, because to say *I am God* is the most blasphemous remark possible to make and also the deepest truth. If you say, *I am God,* meaning Christopher Isherwood is God, this is ludicrous. But if you say that the essential nature which abides behind this apparent personality in myself, is God, this is a statement of the deepest truth, and samadhi is a state in which this truth is known, and not only temporarily known, but known in such a way that once known, the entire man is transformed by the knowledge. We find records that samadhi occurred in the lives of many Christian saints and of saints of all the different religions; there being absolutely no distinction in this respect. Any one cult of a divine being, devotedly followed, must lead to the same result, since there is only one truth and many paths to it.

But in the case of Sri Ramakrishna, this state of samadhi became of almost daily occurrence, and this is something that is of course quite, quite out of the ordinary, even in dealing with figures of this spiritual magnitude.

It is not necessary for me to dwell at length on the actual life of Sri Ramakrishna, because there are many books about it. It's exceedingly simple, exceedingly easy to remember in its external events. He was born in 1836 in a small village in Bengal of peasant parents. He lived exactly fifty years, died in 1886, and his whole life was spent in Bengal, with the exception of a couple of not very long pilgrimages. His parents were extremely devout, and he seems to have been surrounded, both in boyhood and indeed throughout his whole life, by love and by people who loved him. As a boy, he was very charming and lively and amusing, and not at all given to studying, but he always captivated everybody and talked them out of any severity toward him. He was very fond of dressing up, for he loved acting and was incredibly skillful as a mimic. In those days they were very strict about purdah—the custom of keeping the ladies of the household in retirement, so that no outside men ever saw them—and there was one man in the locality who used to boast that nobody had ever seen his womenfolk at all, outside of the family. So Ramakrishna who was in his early teens dressed up as a market woman, went around to the house, sold them some things, gossiped with the various women of the household, and the next day stunned this man by describing to him exactly what each of them had been wearing and what they had said.

When he was in his late teens, he went to Calcutta where his elder brother had a school, a Sanskrit school, but he didn't settle there to learning much. And then a lady who lived in the neighborhood, an enormously wealthy woman named the Rani Rasmani, decided to build a temple on the river bank to the Mother of the Universe. Ramakrishna's elder brother was asked to be the priest in this temple, and he took Ramakrishna along to help him. And so it came about that by the time Ramakrishna was twenty he was settled at this place, which is called Dakshineswar, and there he spent almost all the rest of his life; that's to say, the next thirty years.

The Rani was a woman of very determined character. On one occasion the British were trying to put a tax on the fishermen in the river, so she bought all of the fishing rights, hung chains across the river, claiming that the traffic disturbed the fishing, and wouldn't let anything operate until the British had taken the tax off. She was always doing things like that. But at the same time, she had the grace to realize what an extraordinary individual Ramakrishna was, and she felt that they were privileged to have him there, and that any eccentricities of his were to be absolutely condoned. This is just as well, because Ramakrishna's behavior became progressively stranger and stranger.

You see, he really wanted to know God, and even in religious circles this is very odd and makes for behavior which to outside people appears to be quite insane, because it has a different frame of reference. After all, everybody can understand one wanting money, or position, or sexual love, because we all want such things. But really to want to know God, to the exclusion of everything else, and to be frantic about it, seemed so odd that many people were seriously concerned about Ramakrishna's sanity at this point.

He was also very firm with the Rani, and on one occasion she was meditating beside him at the shrine and started to think about a lawsuit in which she was engaged. Ramakrishna had at that time telepathic powers and turning to her said, "How dare you think such thoughts here!" and smacked her. However, all of this she accepted and realized that they were in the presence of an extraordinary person, a spiritual genius.

And it must be said that throughout all of this period, whenever genuine holy men, people of real spiritual attainment met Ramakrishna, they never thought that he was mad. It was only worldly people who thought so.

Ramakrishna then entered upon a period of about twelve years, during which he went through very elaborate spiritual disciplines under the guidance of two teachers. The first was a woman, who is usually known simply as the Brahmani, and the second was a man, named Totapuri. At the end of this period and during the last twenty years of his life, he began to have many visitors—some of them famous. There was, for example, Keshab Sen, who was one of the great religious leaders in India at that time and was conducting a kind of reformist movement to bring Hinduism more into line with modern times and destroy some of its old customs which he regarded as abuses, such as the caste system, child marriage, etc. Keshab was a genuinely great man in his way, but a man who necessarily was deeply immersed in worldly affairs—he had even visited England and been presented to Queen Victoria—Keshab nevertheless recognized and proclaimed the greatness of Ramakrishna and kept constantly coming to see him at the temple at Dakshineswar.

Then, there also came to him the young men who were later to be his monastic disciples and who were to found the Ramakrishna Order, which exists to this day and of which the Vedanta Society is a branch. The two greatest of them were Brahmananda and Vivekananda. Vivekananda came to this country at the end of the last century and after a very successful and impressive series of lectures all over the country he founded a center in New York. As a direct result of this, a link was established with the head monastery back in Calcutta, so that in due course other groups in other parts of the United States requested that a swami should be sent to them, in order that they could form a center and receive teaching. As early as 1903 there was a center in San Francisco, and then by degrees other centers grew up, including the one in Los Angeles; and so the movement has steadily spread.

But of course, one must remember that what we have here in the States is only a tiny part of the Ramakrishna movement. In India it is a very big order indeed, with many monasteries, not to mention schools, hospitals, and colleges, and centers all over the country.

There are few figures in the whole of religious literature who are as well documented as Ramakrishna. His sayings, his teachings, the whole impression that he made as an individual—everything is conveyed to us in two extraordinary books. One of them is the so-called *Gospel of Sri Ramakrishna* by a man who signs himself simply as "M"—Mahendra. He attended Sri

Ramakrishna during his last period when he had a great many disciples and was constantly in conversation with them, being asked questions and giving answers. M. wrote down everything that was said on every occasion he was present, which makes a book which is of course repetitive, but of fascinating interest. You get from it the atmosphere of complete informality which surrounded Ramakrishna. And you see in his conversation how simplicity was coupled with an extraordinary subtlety. He could answer the most complicated questions in a very simple way, showing great intellectual grasp and yet using the language of a peasant with homely illustrations based, as many of Christ's were, on the life of the countryside.

The other book which is basic to an understanding of Ramakrishna, and which I think is even more wonderful, is a book written by one of his monastic disciples, Swami Saradananda. Saradananda's book is called *Ramakrishna, the Great Master.* It began just as a series of articles which the swami wrote for his disciples late in life, long after Sri Ramakrishna had passed away. But I think that this book conveys in a way in which no other writing does, the extraordinary mixture of simplicity, fun, and strangeness which was in Ramakrishna. Here we are dealing with someone very, very strange; we are in the presence of a tremendous mystery.

Among the many people who saw Ramakrishna, there were some great sages, men who would correspond in our culture to the most responsible leaders of the Christian Church, except that of course in India there is no church in our sense of the word. These men expressed it as their considered opinion, that Ramakrishna was not a human being, but an incarnation of God. And this was said in a country where such statements are not made lightly, or for emotional or dramatic effect, but have an exact, clearly defined significance. When a Hindu talks about a divine incarnation, he means somebody who is the actual vehicle by which God himself appears, manifests himself on the earth. Such a being has no past, he is not subject to the wheel of birth and rebirth—he has no karma in this sense, he simply manifests himself to do good to the world. He is, if you like, an expression of the world's need at any particular moment. He manifests himself and gives through himself power, which is then transmitted and gradually begins to work within society.

Now, of course, it is impossible for us to realize the scope and nature of spiritual power. We think of power in terms of building up something—a big organization—something of this sort; whereas of course the organization, although it inevitably occurs, is really just a by-product. What the power of a figure like Ramakrishna consists in is this, that he could really by his touch, by his physical touch, communicate spiritual knowledge to the people around him, and when he was dying—he had a throat cancer—when he was in a condition in which most people would be scarcely conscious, and would be certainly obsessed by their own suffering; at this very moment he blessed the people around him so that they went into ecstasy, and at this very moment he declared himself, and said, "Yes, he who was Rama and he who was Krishna is present here in this body." You will find a parallel situation in the Christian story when Christ in agony, bleeding on the cross, turned to the thief and said, "Today shalt thou be with me in paradise." He, there, in the same way, was announcing his nonhuman quality, announcing that he was a son of God.

And this surely is what really matters. Nothing else does. I am told that nowadays the room where Ramakrishna lived at Dakshineswar is well kept and you can go there and pay homage, but I rather like a story, accurate or not, which a traveler tells in a book I was reading the other day, of going to Dakshineswar—I suppose in the early 1920s, at a time when the temple was deserted, when Ramakrishna's room was littered, untidy, and uncared for, and the whole place was in a terrible state, and this traveler claims that he spoke to a monk who was around the place and said, "How can you leave the Master's dwelling place in such bad condition," and the monk said, "The

Master isn't here. He's over there, on the other side of the river at the monastery. That's where he is alive. That's where you will find him." Which brings us to the thought that Ramakrishna can be every bit as much alive right here in California, as he is over in India, amongst the scenes of his life on earth.

THE HOME OF RAMAKRISHNA

I am now engaged in trying to write a small introductory book about the life of Sri Ramakrishna, and I naturally felt that, before starting work on it, I must see the places where he lived. So this was the chief object of a trip around the world, from which I've just returned.

We flew to Hawaii, stopped there a few days, and then went on to Japan where we spent almost a month; then down to Hong Kong and took a boat which went down the coast of Java to Bali and then back eventually to Singapore. From Singapore we flew to Bangkok and went over to see the ruins of Angkor; then to Calcutta by air.

Most unfortunately, while I was in Bangkok I got quite sick, with the result that our stay in India was very brief. I made up my mind to see everything I had come to see in the area around Calcutta—that is to say everything connected with the life of Ramakrishna—and then to cut out the rest of the Indian trip and fly directly to London.

So what I saw of India you could put in a thimble and from one point of view it wasn't even fairly representative. India's dearest friends seem mostly to agree that Calcutta is the dirtiest and most depressing city in the country. This is not the fault of the municipal authorities; it is simply because enormous quantities of refugees have come in from East Pakistan. In Hong Kong also, through no fault of the authorities, there is appalling overcrowding, a kind of overcrowding which is almost reminiscent of Dante's hell, with people sleeping all over the sidewalks and the floors of courts and, in fact, hardly having room for the little mat which is their one possession and abode.

Calcutta is very much a city in transition. One facet of the Indian genius, I think is an intelligent tolerance which is the result of a real historical perspective. I remarked to the person who was guiding us around—one of the swamis—on the number of statues of not even at all distinguished or interesting British generals and statesmen which still stand around the streets and parks. I said, "Surely you want to tear those things down, don't you?" He said, "Well, we did remove one or two to begin with, but then we reflected that after all, this was a historical phase in India's development, and they should be kept there as a reminder of that phase." This I thought was truly admirable.

After I had recovered from the first attack of my illness, we went to stay at the Belur Math, the headquarters of the Ramakrishas Order. What I had not expected was the spaciousness of the whole place, and the pleasant parklike quality of the grounds which run right along the edge of the river. I was also very agreeably surprised by the temple. Although I had seen photographs of it, I had always had dark forebodings that a building which attempted to be, as this does, a combination of Gothic, Oriental, and Muslim architecture, couldn't possibly be anything but a rather absurd hybrid. But, after close inspection, I think it really is a very beautiful building of noble proportions, especially inside. The singing and the music in the temple is of wonderful beauty and dramatic power, and it was a very exciting experience at vespers to sit among the monks and be a part of this.

A person who made a most vivid impression upon me, was the swami, who, I believe, for almost twelve years has been uninterruptedly doing the worship. This swami has in fact almost no time to do anything else at all. The schedule of service to Ramakrishna begins for him about four o'clock in the morning and continues until late at night. He has the barest minimum of time for the necessary washing, changes of clothes, food, and sleep. And day after day this service continues. The way in which this devotion expresses itself outwardly is in the exquisite grace with which the swami performs his ritual movements before the shrine. It is a grace which is so unselfconscious, that in other circumstances it would usually be described as animal; but it is of course spiritual, or let us say animal-spiritual without being in any sense egotistic. It is like a dance which is performed without the consciousness of being a dancer, and certainly without the least consciousness of being watched by other people.

Another great experience for me while staying at the math was to meet its head, Swami Sankarananda, a figure of real majesty and kindness. He had recently been in New Delhi for the dedication of a new temple there and while there had fallen and sprained his ankle. When I was brought in to see him, I of course immediately said I was so sorry that this had happened. To this he replied that we must never regard anything that happens to us as a misfortune, but rather as an opportunity for deeper insight, fuller understanding, more complete acceptance of God's will; and he spoke beautifully and touchingly about this for a considerable time. Swami Sankarananda's room is right next to the one which was occupied by Vivekananda during the last years of his life, and this seemed to me wonderful and right that the visible head of the order and its invisible inspirer should be, as it were, side by side under one roof.

Belur Math stands on the bank of the river Hugli, which is the most important of the several mouths of the Ganges. The river at this point is wide and brown, and its tides flow strongly. Across on the other bank you see a low line of palm trees and tropical vegetation, with old houses and gardens facing the water. Almost opposite the math is the ghat at which Sri Ramakrishna was cremated. The view is unfortunately disfigured by the smokestacks of a factory.

But at sunrise and sunset, the river becomes beautifully mysterious, with its outlines dimmed in a murky golden haze. High-prowed boats emerge silently from it. In silhouette, they look a little like gondolas, and indeed I was struck by the resemblance of this golden half-light to that of the sunset on the lagoon at Venice. In the films we shot of both places, the color looks almost identical. As you look up the river from the math you see a large metal bridge. This bridge used to be named for Lord Willingdon, a former viceroy. It is now renamed the Vivekananda Bridge, a measure of the public acceptance and the growing importance of the order in India. The bridge is most unfortunately placed, because it hides what would otherwise be the most dramatic feature of the view—the temple of Dakshineswar which stands just on the other side of the bridge, on the opposite bank.

As at Belur, so also Dakshineswar, where Sri Ramakrishna lived many years as a priest, I was surprised by the size of the grounds. In the photographs it looks as though the row of Shiva temples were very close to the great main mass of the Kali temple which rises above it, but in fact there is a very spacious courtyard behind the riverfront of the small Shiva temples, with the Kali temple rising majestically in the middle of it. All around the courtyard is a colonnade.

Dakshineswar is not so well kept or so orderly as Belur Math. Although people are admitted freely to the grounds of Belur Math during the daytime, there are no beggars, and no one annoys anyone else. People bathe from the bathing ghat, or worship before the shrines, or lie quietly on the grass and talk to their friends. Whereas, at Dakshineswar there is a good deal of interference with the visitor—crowds of children and demands for money—and the surface of the courtyard is rough and broken, making it unpleasant to walk shoeless, which one has to, out of reverence for the holiness of the spot.

Sri Ramakrishna's room is large and pleasant, and is in fact the very best room that he could have been given in the whole temple building. It is on a corner of the colonnade with a view of the Ganges, and is relatively cool, being wide open to the courtyard on the one side and to the riverfront porch on the other side. It has recently been repaved, which many people feel is a great pity, since one no longer has the experience of walking on the actual floor that Sri Ramakrishna trod. Also the original furniture of the room has been added to by many sacred pictures around the walls; one would of course prefer to see the place as it was originally. From this room you see the nahabat, the music tower, in the bottom of which Holy Mother spent so much time, and if Sri Ramakrishna's room was larger than I expected, the room in which Holy Mother lived really shocked me, as it must shock everybody who sees it, by its smallness. It seems incredible that this little circular chamber could house not only one, but sometimes two or three people, and that Holy Mother could have lived there so long and cooked there and remained often during the day, as was customary at that time in complete seclusion, presumably with the doors shut. The heat must have been frightful.

Beyond this music tower you come to the famous tree, the Panchavati, under which Sri Ramakrishna used to meditate. There again was something that disconcerted me, and that was the stone platform under the tree, but Swami Prabhavananda tells me that this is customary. They always have such a platform. In my romantic way, I had imagined Sri Ramakrishna meditating right on the ground—I suppose because that would have been more like the Buddha meditating in the forest. A little of what I suppose used to be the atmosphere of Dakshineswar remained in that there was a religious madman who wandered about while we were there both times, shouting and chanting, and crying out the names of God, much as you read of the characters who did that in Ramakrishna's day. On beyond there, the grove which used to exist has been cut down and there is a large open lot, of no particular interest.

Also in Calcutta we visited the Cossipore garden house. That has been very largely restored, of course, and is not really the same place, except that it is said to look identical and it stands in exactly the same position.

To the Westerner, coming to these sacred spots and anxious of course to have some kind of emotional experience, there is a quality in Oriental architecture which perhaps defeats him— perhaps this is good, not bad at all—and that is the openness of everything. In America and in Europe one is accustomed to think of atmosphere as something you catch in a box. You go into a little room where a great man died, or was born, and you feel a kind of concentration of something which is bottled in there and can't get out. In India this is really not possible because of the opensidedness of things, and so far as one's surface emotions or surface romanticism goes, it's a great deal harder to feel that I am here and not someplace else, that I am absolutely within something, because you're in most cases at least one-quarter out of doors.

After we had been around Calcutta and seen a number of houses which Ramakrishna used to visit, we made the excursion out to the birthplaces of Sri Ramakrishna and of Holy Mother; that is to say, Kamarpukur and Jayrambati. We also visited Surmanagar, the native village of Swami Prabhavananda, and I had the great happiness of meeting his three brothers and other members of his family.

This trip out to the villages was also a journey from 1958 right back to the days of Ramakrishna because, as the swami who accompanied us told us, there have been in these small villages almost no outward changes during the past hundred years. Some of the boys now wear shorts instead of dhotis, and the older girls no longer veil their faces on the street—that is all.

We began by going by train to Bankura, where there is one of the many Ramakrishna centers. We had a first-class sleeper, which was actually more like a freight car with beds in it. I never thought that beds could be too well sprung, but we all three, the swami and my friend and I, bounced all night through endless shuntings and stops. Nevertheless, we had the satisfaction of having traveled deluxe, and of having been most respectfully seen off at Howrah station by the station master himself. It's very noticeable, incidentally, the great attention and reverence paid to the swamis in India, or at least certainly in the Calcutta area. I was enormously impressed by something which perhaps I ought not to have been impressed by, and that was the genuine disinterestedness and lack of vanity with which the swamis received the almost continuous reverence which was shown to them.

I was greatly impressed by the apparent ease with which individual swamis can pass from periods of contemplative or ritualistic life to very down-to-earth social service; the running of clinics and of schools, the keeping of accounts, and even the doing of quite menial work. This is indeed a proof of the completeness of their self-dedication.

To return to the villages—the Bengal countryside is not particularly charming in December; somewhat bare and eroded. The paddy fields are dried out, with only a short stubble coming up through the earth. A great deal of red dust blows about the gently undulating countryside. The villages themselves form little oases with clumps of palms and banyans, and some fruit trees. The houses are thatched and often the village street is too narrow for the bullock carts to pass each other. There will be one or more tanks for bathing and washing clothes—in my ignorance before coming to India I supposed a tank must be like a swimming pool, paved at the bottom, but they are actually not in most cases, just dug-out village ponds. I think that possibly Jayrambati is less changed from the days of Holy Mother than is Kamarpukur, because in the case of Kamarpukur there has been some rebuilding to meet the needs of the pilgrims. Again and again, looking at the children of those two villages, these very slender, bright-eyed, rather mischievous, laughing children, one said to oneself, "One of those could have been he." It's very easy to imagine Gadadhar there in that setting.

India is a marvelous country and a very romantic one; but it is romantic in the wrong sense to suppose that you can go there and maintain such a continuously high spiritual mood that you are unaware of the trials of the climate. And, in addition, you will be lucky if you don't get at least slightly sick! I am very happy to be working on my book in these temperate Californian surroundings, and not in the heat of the tropics.

On the other hand, it is undoubtedly a great grace and a great privilege to have been able to visit these places. And I firmly believe that everybody who does so must receive some kind of deep spiritual radiations, even if he is utterly unaware of it at the time. I myself will never forget the vivid impressions of my short visit; and the boundless kindness of the swamis at the Belur Math and elsewhere.

ON SWAMI VIVEKANANDA

One morning early in September 1893, a lady named Mrs. George W. Hale looked out through a window of her handsome home on Chicago's Dearborn Avenue and saw, seated on the opposite side of the street, a young man of Oriental appearance who was dressed in a turban and the ochre robe of a Hindu monk.

Mrs. Hale was, fortunately, not a conventional woman. She did not call the police to tell the stranger to move on; she did not even ring for the servants to go and ask him what he wanted. She noticed that he was unshaven and that his clothes were crumpled and dirty, but she was aware, also, that there was a kind of royal air about him. There he sat, perfectly composed, meditative, serene. He did not look as if he had lost his way. (And, indeed, he was quite the opposite of lost, for he had just resigned himself to the will of God.) Mrs. Hale suddenly made a most intelligent guess; coming out of her house and crossing the street, she asked him politely, "Sir, are you a delegate to the Parliament of Religions?"

She was answered with equal politeness, in fluent, educated English. The stranger introduced himself as Swami Vivekananda and told her that he had indeed come to Chicago to attend the meetings of the Parliament, although he was not officially a delegate. As a matter of fact, he had first arrived in Chicago from India in the middle of July, only to find that the Parliament's opening had been postponed till September. His money was running short, and someone had advised him that he would be able to live more cheaply in Boston, so he had taken the train there. On the train, he had met a lady who had invited him to stay at her home, which was called "Breezy Meadows." Since then, he had given talks to various church and social groups, been asked a lot of silly questions about his country, been laughed at by children because of his funny clothes. The day before yesterday, Professor J. H. Wright, who taught Greek at Harvard University, had bought him a ticket back to Chicago, assuring him that he would be welcome at the Parliament, even though he had no invitation: "To ask you, Swami, for credentials is like asking the sun if it has permission to shine." The professor had also given him the address of the committee which was in charge of the delegates to the Parliament, but this address Vivekananda somehow lost on his way to Chicago. He tried to get information from passersby on the street but, as ill luck would have it, the station was situated in the midst of a district where German was chiefly spoken, and the swami could not make himself understood.

Meanwhile, night was coming on. The swami did not know how to obtain or use a city directory and so was at a loss how to find a suitable hotel. It seemed to him simpler to sleep in a big empty boxcar in the freight yards of the railroad. Next morning, hungry and rumpled, he woke, as he put it, "smelling fresh water," and had begun to walk in a direction which brought him, sure enough, to the edge of Lake Michigan. But the wealthy homes of Lake Shore Drive proved inhospitable; he had knocked at the doors of several and had been rudely turned away. At length, after further wanderings, he had found himself here, and had decided to go no farther but to sit down and await whatever event God might send. And now, Vivekananda concluded, "What a romantic deliverance! How strange are the ways of the Lord!"

Mrs. Hale must have laughed as she listened to this; for Vivekananda always related his adventures and misadventures with humor, and his own deep chuckles were most infectious. They went back together into the house, where the swami was invited to wash and shave and eat breakfast. Mrs. Hale then accompanied him to the headquarters of the committee, which arranged for his accommodation with the other Oriental delegates to the Parliament.

The idea of holding a Parliament of Religions in Chicago had been conceived at least five years before this, in relation to the main project of the World's Columbian Exposition, which was to be held to commemorate the four hundredth anniversary of the discovery of America by Columbus. The exposition was designed to demonstrate western man's material progress, especially in science and technology. It was agreed, however, that all forms of progress must be represented, and there were congresses devoted to such varied themes as woman's progress, the public press, medicine and surgery, temperance, commerce and finance, music, government and legal reform, economic science, and—strange as it may sound to us nowadays—Sunday rest. And since, to quote the official language of the committee, "faith in a Divine Power has been, like the sun, a light-giving and fructifying potency in Man's intellectual and moral development," there had also to be a Parliament of Religions.

One may smile at all the pomposity, but it must be agreed that the calling of such a parliament was a historic act of liberalism. This was probably the first time in the history of the world that representatives of all the major religions had been brought together in one place, with freedom to express their beliefs. Paradoxically, the most genuinely liberal of the Parliament's organizers were the agnostics; for they were interested solely in promoting interreligious tolerance. The zealous Christians took a less impartial view, as was only to be expected. In the words of a Catholic priest: "It is not true that all religions are equally good; but neither is it true that all religions except one are no good at all. The Christianity of the future, more just than that of the past, will assign to each its place in that work of evangelical preparation which the elder doctors of the

Church discern in heathenism itself, and which is not yet completed." In other words, heathenism has its uses as a preparation for Christianity.

But what really mattered was the acceptance of an invitation to preside at the Parliament by Cardinal Gibbons, leader of the American Catholics. This was all the more valuable because the Archbishop of Canterbury had refused to attend, objecting that the very meeting of such a parliament implied the equality of all religions. In addition to the Christians, the Buddhists, the Hindus, the Moslems, the Jews, the Confucianists, the Shintoists, the Zoroastrians, and a number of smaller sects and groups were represented. Vivekananda could, of course, be counted as a recruit to the Hindu delegation; but in fact, as we shall see, he was standing for something larger than any one sect; the ancient Indian doctrine of the universality of spiritual truth.

When the Parliament opened, on the morning of September 11, Vivekananda immediately attracted notice as one of the most striking figures seated on the platform, with his splendid robe, yellow turban, and handsome bronze face. In his photographs, one is struck by the largeness of his features—they have something of the lion about them—the broad strong nose, the full expressive lips, the great dark burning eyes. Eyewitnesses were also impressed by the majesty of his presence. Though powerfully built, Vivekananda was not above medium height, but he seems always to have created the effect of bigness. It was said of him that, despite his size, he moved with a natural masculine grace; "like a great cat," as one lady expressed it. In America, he was frequently taken for an Indian prince or aristocrat, because of his quiet but assured air of command.

Others commented on his look of being "inly pleased"; he seemed able to draw upon inner reserves of strength at all times, and there was a humorous, watchful gleam in his eyes which suggested calm, amused detachment of spirit. Everyone responded to the extraordinarily deep, bell-like beauty of his voice; certain of its vibrations caused a mysterious psychic excitement among his hearers. And no doubt this had something to do with the astonishing reaction of the audience to Vivekananda's first speech.

During that first morning's session, Vivekananda's turn came to speak; but he excused himself and asked for more time. Later, in a letter to friends in India, he confessed that he had been suffering from stage fright. All the other delegates had prepared addresses; he had none. However, this hesitation only increased the general interest in him.

At length, during the afternoon, Vivekananda rose to his feet. In his deep voice, he began, "Sisters and Brothers of America"—and the entire audience, many hundred people, clapped and cheered wildly for two whole minutes. Hitherto, the audience had certainly been well disposed; some of the speakers had been greeted enthusiastically and all of them with sufficient politeness. But nothing like this demonstration had taken place. No doubt the vast majority of those present hardly knew why they had been so powerfully moved. The appearance, even the voice, of Vivekananda cannot fully explain it. A large gathering has its own strange kind of subconscious telepathy, and this one must have been somehow aware that it was in the presence of that most unusual of all beings, a man whose words express exactly what he is. When Vivekananda said, "Sisters and Brothers," he actually meant that he regarded the American women and men before him as his sisters and brothers: the well-worn oratorical phrase became simple truth.

As soon as they would let him, the swami continued his speech. It was quite a short one, pleading for universal tolerance and stressing the common basis of all religions. When it was over, there was more, thunderous applause. A lady who was present recalled later, "I saw scores of women walking over to the benches to get near him, and I said to myself, 'Well, my lad, if you can resist that onslaught you are indeed a God!'" Such onslaughts were to become a part of the daily discipline of Vivekananda's life in America.

He made several more speeches during the days that followed, including an important statement of the nature and ideals of Hinduism. By the time the Parliament had come to an end, he was, beyond comparison, its most popular speaker. He had his pick of social invitations. A lecture bureau offered to organize a tour for him; and he accepted.

In those days, when the frontier was still a living memory, one did not have to go far from the great cities to find oneself in the pioneer world of the tent show. Politicians, philosophers, writers, the great actress Sarah Bernhardt herself—all were treated more or less as circus attractions. Even today, the name "Swami" is associated with theatrical trickery, and most Americans are quite unaware that those who have the right to call themselves by it have taken formal monastic vows; that it is, in fact, a title just as worthy of respect as that of "Father" in the Catholic church. Vivekananda called himself Swami, and therefore, in the eyes of the public, he was regarded as some kind of an entertainer; he might hope for applause, but he could expect no consideration for his privacy. He had to face the crudest publicity, the most brutal curiosity, hospitality which was lavish but ruthless and utterly exhausting. It exhausted him and eventually wrecked his health but, for the time being, he was equal to it and even seemed to enjoy it. He was outspoken to the point of bluntness, never at a loss for repartee, never thrown off balance even when he roared with momentary indignation because of some idiotic question about his "heathen" countrymen. No one could laugh at him as he laughed at himself; for no one else could appreciate the rich and subtle joke of his very presence in these surroundings—a monk preaching in a circus!

Vivekananda had come to America to speak for his native land. He wanted to tell Americans about India's poverty and appeal for their help. But he also had a message to the West. He asked his hearers to forsake their materialism and learn from the ancient spirituality of the Hindus. What he was working for was an exchange of values. He recognized great virtues in the

West—energy and initiative and courage—which he found lacking among Indians; and he had not come to America in a spirit of negative criticism. It is significant that when, during the earliest days of his visit, he was taken to see a prison near Boston, his reaction was as follows:

> How benevolently the inmates are treated, how they are reformed and sent back as useful members of society—how grand, how beautiful, you must see to believe! And on, how my heart ached to think of what we think of the poor, the low, in India. They have no chance, no escape, no way to climb up. They sink lower and lower every day.

Yet he offended many by his outspokenness. "In New York," he used to say smilingly, "I have emptied entire halls." And no wonder! To the ears of rigid fundamentalists, his teaching of man's essential divinity must have sounded utterly blasphemous, especially as it was presented in his picturesque, seriocomic phrases: "Look at the ocean and not at the wave; see no difference between ant and angel. Every worm is the brother of the Nazarene. . . . Obey the Scriptures until you are strong enough to do without them. . . . Every man in Christian countries has a huge cathedral on his head, and on top of that a book. . . . The range of idols is from wood and stone to Jesus and Buddha. . . . "

Vivekananda taught that God is within each one of us, and that each one of us was born to rediscover his own God-nature. His favorite story was of a lion who imagined himself to be a sheep, until another lion showed him his reflection in a pool. "And you are lions," he would tell his hearers, "you are pure, infinite, and perfect souls. . . . He, for whom you have been weeping and praying in churches and temples . . . is your own Self." He was the prophet of self-reliance, of individual search and effort.

He spoke little about the cults of Hinduism—the particular devotion to Rama, Kali, Vishnu, or Krishna which is practiced by the devotees of the various sects. It was only occasionally that Vivekananda referred to his own personal cult and revealed that he, too, had a master whom he regarded as a divine incarnation—a master named Ramakrishna, who had died less than ten years previously, and whom he himself had intimately known.

Vivekananda was a very great devotee; but he did not proclaim his devotion to all comers. His refusal to do so was a considered decision. He said: "I preached Ramakrishna's principles. If people accept the principles, they will eventually accept the personality."

At the time of the Parliament of Religions, Vivekananda was only thirty years old; he had been born in Calcutta on January 12, 1863. The name of his family was Datta, and his parents gave him the name Narendranath; Naren for short. As a monk, he had wandered about India under various names; he assumed the name of Vivekananda only just before embarking for the United States, at the suggestion of the Maharaja of Khetri, who, with the Maharaja of Mysore, paid the expenses of his journey. *Viveka* is a Sanskrit word meaning discrimination, more particularly in the philosphic sense of discrimination between the real (God) and the unreal (the phenomena recognized by our sense perceptions). *Ananda* means divine bliss, or the peace which is obtained through enlightenment; it is a frequently used suffix to any name which is assumed by a monk.

When Naren was in his middle teens, he started going to college in Calcutta. He was a good-looking, athletic youth and extremely intelligent. He was also a fine singer and could play several musical instruments. Already, he showed a great power for leadership among the boys of his own age. His teachers felt sure that he was destined to make a mark in life.

At that period, Calcutta was the chief port of entry for European ideas and cultural influences; and no young Indian student could remain unaffected by them. To meet the challenge of missionary Christianity, a movement had been formed to modernize Hinduism—to do away with ancient ritual and priestcraft, to emancipate women, and to abolish child marriage. This movement was called the Brahmo Samaj. Naren joined it but soon found its aims superficial; they did not satisfy his own spiritual needs. He read Hume, Herbert Spencer, and John Stuart Mill and began to call himself an agnostic. His parents urged him to marry, but he refused, feeling that he must remain chaste and unattached so as to be ready to devote himself body and soul to a great cause. What cause? He did not yet exactly know. He was still looking for someone and something in which he could wholeheartedly believe. Meanwhile, his restless and fearless spirit was on fire for action.

It so happened that a relative of Naren's was a devotee of Ramakrishna, and that one of Naren's teachers, Professor Hastie, was among the few Englishmen who had ever met him. What these two had to say about Ramakrishna excited Naren's curiosity. Then, in November 1881, he was invited to sing at a house where Ramakrishna was a guest. They had a brief conversation and Ramakrishna invited the young man to come and visit him at the Dakshineswar Temple, on the Ganges a few miles outside Calcutta, where he lived.

From the first, Naren was intrigued and puzzled by Ramakrishna's personality. He had never met anyone quite like this slender, bearded man in his middle forties who had the innocent directness of a child. He had about him an air of intense delight, and he was perpetually crying aloud or bursting into song to express his joy, his joy in God the Mother Kali, who evidently existed for him as a live presence. Ramakrishna's talk was a blend of philosophical subtlety and homely parable. He spoke with a slight stammer, in the dialect of his native Bengal village, and sometimes used coarse farmyard words with the simple frankness of a peasant. By this time, his fame had spread, and many distinguished Bengalis were his constant visitors, including Keshab Sen, the leader of the Brahmo Samaj. Keshab loved and admired Ramakrishna in spite of his own reformist principles; for Ramakrishna was a ritualist and an orthodox Hindu, and Keshab's social concern seemed to him merely an amusing and necessarily fruitless game. The world, according to a Hindu saying, is like the curly tail of a dog—how can you ever straighten it out?

So Naren went to Dakshineswar with a divided mind—half of him eager for self-dedication and devotion; the other, Western-educated half, skeptical, impatient of superstition. When Naren and a few of his friends came into Ramakrishna's room, Ramakrishna asked him to sing. Naren did so. The extraordinary scene which followed can best be described in his words:

Well, I sang that song, and then, soon after, he suddenly rose, took me by the hand and led me out on to the porch north of his room, shutting the door behind him. It was locked from the outside, so we were alone. I thought he was going to give me some advice in private. But, to my utter amazement, he began shedding tears of joy—floods of them—as he held my hand, and talking to me tenderly, as if to an old friend. "Ah!" he said, "you've come so late! How could you be so unkind—keeping me waiting so long? My ears are almost burnt off, listening to the talk of worldly people. Oh, how I've longed to unburden my heart to someone who can understand everything—my innermost experience!" He went on like this, amidst his sobbing. And then he folded his palms and addressed me solemnly, "Lord I know you! You are Nara, the ancient sage, the incarnation of Narayana. You have come to earth to take away the sorrows of mankind . . . " And so forth.

I was absolutely dumbfounded by his behaviour. "Who is this man I've come to see?" I said to myself. "He must be raving mad! Why, I'm nobody—the son of Vishwanath Datta—and he dares to call me Nara!" But I kept quiet and let him go on. Presently he went back into his room and brought me out some sweets—sugar candy and butter; and he fed me with his own hands. I kept telling him, "Please give them to me—I want to share them with my friends," but it was no good. He wouldn't stop until I'd eaten all of them. Then he seized me by the hand and said, "Promise me you'll come back here alone, soon!" He was so pressing that I had to say yes. Then I went back with him to join my friends.

This was certainly a searching psychological test for an eighteen-year-old college intellectual! But Naren's intuition went much deeper than his sophistication. he was unable to dismiss Ramakrishna from his mind as a mere eccentric. If this man was mad, then even his madness was somehow holy; Naren felt that he had been in the presence of a great saint, and already he began to love him.

At their second meeting, Ramakrishna revealed himself in a quite different aspect, as a being endowed with supernatural and terrifying power. This time, Naren found him alone in his room. He greeted Naren affectionately and asked him to sit down beside him. Then, as Naren described it later:

Muttering something to himself, with his eyes fixed on me, he slowly drew near me . . . In the twinkling of an eye, he placed his right foot on my body. At his touch, I had an entirely new experience. With my eyes wide open, I saw that the walls and everything else in the room were whirling around, vanishing into nothingness; the whole universe, together with my own individuality, was about to be lost in an all-encompassing, mysterious Void! I was terribly frightened and thought I must be facing death—for the loss of my individuality meant nothing less than that to me. I couldn't control myself: I cried out, "What are you doing to me! I have my parents at home!" At this, he laughed aloud. Stroking my chest, he said, "All right, that's enough for now. Everything will come in time." The wonderful thing was, as soon as he'd said that, the whole experience came to an end. I was myself again. And everything inside and outside the room was just as it had been before.

Ramakrishna had, by his touch, taken Naren to the very brink of that superconscious experience which the Hindus call *samadhi*. In samadhi, all sense of personal identity vanishes and the real Self, the indwelling Godhead, is known. The Godhead, being a unity, is experienced as a sort of Void, in contrast to the multiplicity of objects which make up our ordinary sense consciousness. Within that Void, personal identity is lost—and loss of identity must necessarily seem, to those who are not prepared for it, like death.

For Ramakrishna, in his almost unimaginably high state of spiritual consciousness, samadhi was a daily experience, and the awareness of God's presence never left him. Vivekananda recalls that, "I crept near him and asked him the question I had been asking others all my life: 'Do you believe in God, sir?' 'Yes,' he replied. 'Can you prove it, sir?' 'Yes.' 'How?' 'Because I see Him just as I see you here, only much more intensely.' That impressed me at once. For the first time, I found a man who dared to say that he saw God, that religion was a reality—to be felt, to be sensed in an infinitely more intense way than we can sense the world."

After this, Naren became a frequent visitor to Dakshineswar. He found himself gradually drawn into the circle of youthful disciples—most of them about his own age—whom Ramakrishna was training to follow the monastic life. But Naren did not yield to this influence easily. He kept asking himself if Ramakrishna's power could not be explained away as hypnotism. He refused, at first, to have anything to do with the worship of Kali, saying that this was mere superstition. And Ramakrishna seemed pleased at his scruples. He used to say: "Test me as the money changers test their coins. You mustn't believe me till you've tested me thoroughly." And, in his turn, he tested Naren, ignoring him for weeks on end to find if this would stop him from coming to Dakshineswar. When it did not, Ramakrishna was delighted and congratulated him on his inner strength. "Anyone else," he said, "would have left me long ago."

Indeed, Naren's temperamental doubt is one of his most inspiring qualities. Doubt is something we have all experienced, and it should reassure us greatly that this keen observer took nothing for granted. It may even seem to us, as we read the life of Ramakrishna and see how often he granted Naren the deepest revelations, that Naren doubted too long and too much. But we must remember that Naren's faith was no facile thing. He doubted greatly because he was capable of believing greatly. For most of us, the consequences of conversion to a belief are not very far-reaching. For Naren, to believe meant absolute self-dedication to the object of his belief. No wonder he hesitated! No wonder his inner struggles were so severe!

In 1885 Ramakrishna developed cancer of the throat. As it became increasingly evident that their Master would not be with them much longer, the young disciples drew more and more closely together. Naren was their leader, together with the boy named Rakhal who later became Swami Brahmananda. One day, when Ramakrishna lay in the last stages of his illness, Naren was meditating in a room downstairs. Suddenly, he lost outward consciousness and went into samadhi. For a moment, he was terrified and cried out, "Where is my body?" Another of the disciples thought he must be dying and ran upstairs to tell their master. "Let him stay that way for a while," said Ramakrishna with a smile, "he has been teasing me to give him this experience long enough." Much later, Naren came into Ramakrishna's room, full of joy and peace. "Now Mother has shown you everything," Ramakrishna told him. "But I shall keep the key. When you have done Mother's work, you will find the treasure again." This was only one of several occasions on which Ramakrishna made it clear that he had destined Naren for a mission of teaching in the world.

On August 16, 1886, Ramakrishna uttered the name of Kali in a clear ringing voice and passed into the final samadhi. At noon next day, the doctor pronounced him dead.

The boys felt that they must hold together, and a devotee found them a house at Baranagore, about halfway between Calcutta and Dakshineswar, which they could use for their monastery. It was a dilapidated old place, with cobras under the floor, which could be rented cheaply because it was supposed to be haunted. Here they installed the ashes of Ramakrishna within a shrine, which they worshiped daily. Encouraged by Naren, they resolved to renounce the world; later they took the monastic vow in the prescribed fashion.

There were only fifteen of them. They had almost no money and few friends. Sometimes they were altogether without food, at others they lived only on boiled rice, salt, and bitter herbs. Each had two pieces of loincloth, nothing more. They owned a set of clothes in common, however, to be worn by anyone who had to go out into the city. They slept on straw mats on the floor. Yet they joked and laughed continually, sang hymns, and engaged in eager philosophic discussions; they were silent only when they meditated. At all times they felt Ramakrishna's presence in their midst. Far from regarding him with awe and sadness, they could even make fun of him. A visitor to the house describes how Naren mimicked Ramakrishna going into ecstasy, while the others roared with laughter.

But gradually the boys became restless for the life of the wandering monk. With staff and begging bowl, they wandered all over India, visiting shrines and places of pilgrimage, preaching, begging, passing months of meditation in lonely huts. Sometimes they were entertained by rajas or wealthy devotees; much more often, they shared the food of the very poor.

Such experiences were particularly valuable to Naren. During the years 1890 to 1893 he acquired the first-hand knowledge of India's hunger, misery, nobility, and spiritual wisdom which he was to carry with him on his journey to the West. After traveling the whole length of the country he reached Cape Comorin, and here he had a vision. He saw that India had a mission in the modern world as a force for spiritual regeneration, but he also saw that this force could not become effective until India's social conditions had been radically improved. Funds must be raised for schools and hospitals; thousands of teachers and workers must be recruited and organized. It was then that he formed his decision to go to the United States in search of help. And this decision was later confirmed when the Raja of Ramnad suggested he should attend the then newly announced Chicago Parliament of Religions. Thus the specific opportunity was related to Naren's general intention. At the end of May 1893 he sailed from Bombay, via Hong Kong and Japan, to Vancouver; from there he went on by train to Chicago.

After the closing of the Parliament of Religions, Vivekananda spent nearly two whole years lecturing in various parts of the eastern and central United States, appearing chiefly in Chicago, Detroit, Boston, and New York. By the spring of 1895 he was desperately weary and in poor health; but, characteristically, he made light of it. "Are you never serious, Swamiji?" someone once asked him, perhaps with a hint of reproach. "Oh yes," he replied, "when I have the belly ache." He could even see the funny side of the many cranks and healers who unmercifully pestered him, hoping to steal a reflection of his glory. In his letters he refers jokingly to "the sect of Mrs. Whirlpool" and to a certain mental healer "of metaphysico-chemico-physico-religioso, what-not."

At the same time he met and made an impression on people of a more serious kind—Robert Ingersoll the agnostic, Nikola Tesla the inventor, Madame Calvé the singer. And, most important of all, he attracted a few students whose interest and enthusiasm were not temporary; who were prepared to dedicate the rest of their lives to the practice of his teaching. In June 1895 he was invited to bring a dozen of these to a house in Thousand Island Park on the St. Lawrence River. Here, for nearly two months, he taught them informally, as Ramakrishna had taught him and his brother disciples. Nobody who was present ever forgot this period, and it must certainly have been much the happiest part of Vivekananda's first visit to America.

In August he sailed for France and England, returning to New York in December. It was then that, at the urgent request of his devotees, he founded the first of the Vedanta Societies in America: the Vedanta Society of New York. "The Ramakrishna Society." It was then, also, that he received two academic offers, the chair of Eastern Philosophy at Harvard and a similar position at Columbia. He declined both, saying that, as a wandering monk, he could not settle down to work of this kind. In any case, he was longing to return to India. In April he sailed for England, which was to be the first stage of his journey home.

From England he took with him two of his most faithful and energetic disciples, Captain and Mrs. Sevier—also J. J. Goodwin, an Englishman whom he had first met in America and who had become the recorder of his lectures and teachings. Later, he was followed to India by Margaret Noble, the Irishwoman who became Sister Nivedita and devoted the rest of her life to the education of Indian women and the cause of India's independence. All of these eventually died in India.

Vivekananda landed in Ceylon in the middle of January 1897. From there on, his journey to Calcutta was a triumphal progress. His countrymen had followed the accounts of his American lectures in the newspapers. Perhaps Vivekananda's success had sometimes been exaggerated. But they quite rightly regarded his visit to the West as a symbolic victory far exceeding in its proportions the mere amount of money had collected for his cause or the number of disciples he had made. Indeed, one may claim that no Indian before Vivekananda had ever made Americans and Englishmen accept him on such terms—not as a subservient ally, not as an avowed opponent, but as a sincere well-wisher and friend, equally ready to teach and to learn, to ask for and to offer help. Who else had stood, as he stood, impartially between East and West, prizing the virtues and condemning the defects of both cultures? Who else could represent in his own person Young India of the nineties in synthesis with Ancient India of the Vedas? Who else could stand forth as India's champion against poverty and oppression and yet sincerely praise American idealism and British singleness of purpose? Such was Vivekananda's greatness.

In the midst of all this adulation, Vivekananda never forgot who he was: the disciple of Ramakrishna and the equal brother of his fellow monks. On May 1, 1897, he called a meeting of the monastic and householder disciples of Ramakrishna in order to establish their work on an organized basis. What Vivekananda proposed was an integration of educational, philanthropic, and religious activities; and it was thus that the Ramakrishna Mission and the Ramakrishna Math, or monastery, came into existence. The Mission went to work immediately, taking part in famine and plague relief and founding its first hospitals and schools. Brahmananda was elected as its president, and to him Vivekananda handed over all the money had had collected in America and Europe. Having done this, he was obliged to ask for a few pennies in order to take the ferryboat across the Ganges. Henceforward, he insisted on sharing the poverty of his brother monks.

The math was consecrated some time later, at Belur, a short distance downriver from Dakshineswar Temple, on the opposite bank of the Ganges. This Belur Math is still the chief monastery of the Ramakrishna Order, which now has nearly a hundred centers in different parts of India and neighboring Asian lands, devoted either to the contemplative life or to social service, or to a combination of both. The Ramakrishna Mission has its own hospitals and dispensaries, its own colleges and high schools, industrial and agricultural schools, libraries and publishing houses, with monks of the order in charge of them.

In June 1899 Vivekananda sailed for a second visit to the Western world, taking with him Nivedita and Swami Turiyananda, one of his brother monks. This time, he went by way of Europe and England, but he spent most of the next year in America. He went to California and left Turiyananda to teach in San Francisco. It was Vivekananda's wish to found a number of Vedanta centers in the West. At the present day, there are ten centers in the United States, one in the Argentine, one in England, and one in France.

By the time he returned to India, Vivekananda was a very sick man; he had said himself that he did not expect to live much longer. Yet he was happy and calm—glad, it seemed, to feel a release from the anxious energy which had driven him throughout his earlier years. Now he longed only for the peace of contemplation. Just before leaving America, he wrote a beautiful and remarkably self-revealing letter to a friend:

I am glad I was born, glad I suffered so, glad I did make big blunders, glad to enter peace. Whether this body will fall and release me or I enter into freedom in the body, the old man is gone, gone for ever, never to come back again! Behind my work was ambition, behind my love was personality, behind my purity was fear. now they are vanishing and I drift.

Some say that Vivekananda's departure from this life, on July 4, 1902, at the Belur Math, had the appearance of a premeditated act. For several months previously, he had been releasing himself from his various responsibilities and training successors. His health was better. He ate his midday meal with relish, talked philosophy, and went for a two-mile walk. In the evening, he passed into deep meditation, and the heart stopped beating. For hours they tried to rouse him. But his work, it seemed, was done, and Ramakrishna had given him back the key to the treasure.

The best introduction to Vivekananda is not, however, to read about him but to read him. The swami's personality, with all its charm and force, its courageousness, its spiritual authority, its fury, and its fun, comes through to you very strongly in his writings and recorded words.

In reading him, it is always well to remember that "a foolish consistency is the hobgoblin of little minds." When Emerson wrote these words in his essay on self-reliance, he was contrasting the "little minds" with the great minds of Jesus, Socrates, and others. No doubt Emerson would have added Vivekananda to his list if they could have met and come to know each other. But he died in 1882.

Vivekananda was the last person in the world to worry

about formal consistency. He almost always spoke extempore, fired by the circumstances of the moment, addressing himself to the condition of a particular group of hearers, reacting to the intent of a certain question. That was his nature—and he was supremely indifferent if his words of today seemed to contradict those of yesterday. As a man of enlightenment, he knew that the truth is never contained in arrangements of sentences. It is within the speaker himself. If what he is, is true, then words are unimportant. In this sense, Vivekananda is incapable of self-contradiction.

Vivekananda was not only a great teacher with an international message; he was also a very great Indian, a patriot and an inspirer of his countrymen down to the present generation. But it is a mistake to think of him as a political figure, even in the best meaning of the word. First and last, he was the boy who dedicated his life to Ramakrishna. His mission was spiritual, not political or even social, in the last analysis.

The policy of the Ramakrishna Order has always been faithful to Vivekananda's intention. In the early twenties, when India's struggle with England had become intense and bitter, the order was harshly criticized for refusing to allow its members to take part in Gandhi's noncooperation movement. But Gandhi himself never joined in this criticism. He understood perfectly that a religious body which supports a political cause— no matter how noble and just—can only compromise itself spiritually and thereby lose that very authority which is its justification for existence within human society. In 1921 Gandhi came to the Belur Math on the anniversary of Vivekananda's birthday and paid a moving tribute to him. The swami's writings, Gandhi said, had taught him to love India even more. He reverently visited the room overlooking the Ganges in which Vivekananda spent the last months of his life.

You can visit that room today; it is still kept exactly as Vivekananda left it. But it does not seem museumlike or even unoccupied. Right next to it is the room which is used by the president of the Ramakrishna Order. There they are, dwelling side by side, the visible human authority and the invisible inspiring presence. In the life of the Belur Math, Vivekananda still lives and is as much a participant in its daily activities as any of its monks.

On the Writings of Swami Vivekananda

"If only we had known him!" we say. Most of us take it for granted that we should be able to recognize a great spiritual teacher if we could meet one. Should we? Probably we flatter ourselves. . . . Still, it must be agreed that a live teacher is vastly preferable to his dead book. Mere printed words can't usually convey the tone of their speaker's voice, much less the spiritual power behind that tone.

But Vivekananda is one of the rare exceptions. Reading *his* printed words, we can catch something of the tone of his voice and even feel some sense of contact with his power. Why is this?

Perhaps because most of these teachings were originally spoken, not written down, by him. They have the informality and urgency of speech. Furthermore, Vivekananda is speaking a language which we can understand but which is nevertheless inimitably his own; Vivekananda-English—that marvelously forceful idiom of quaintly turned phrases and explosive exclamations. It recreates his personality for us even now, three-quarters of a century later.

Vivekananda's directness is disconcerting. He points his finger straight at you—like Uncle Sam in the old recruiting posters. There can be no pretending to yourself that he is talking to somebody else. He means *you* and you had better listen.

You had better listen, says Vivekananda, because you do not know who you are. You imagine that you are Mr. or Ms. Jones.

That is your fundamental, fatal mistake. Your opinion of yourself, be it high or low, is also mistaken; but that is of secondary importance. You may strut through life as the Emperor Jones or crawl through it as Jones the slave; it makes no difference. The Emperor Jones, if there were such a creature, would have subjects; the slave Jones would have a master. You have neither. For you are Brahman, eternal God, and, wherever you look, you see nothing but Brahman, wearing the many million disguises which are called by names as absurd as your own— Jones, Juarez, Jinnah, Jung, Jocho, Janvier, Jagatai, Jablochov; names which all mean the same thing, *I am not you*.

You do not know who you are because you are living in ignorance. This ignorance may seem pleasurable at moments, but essentially it is a state of bondage and therefore misery. Your misery arises from the fact that Jones, as Jones, has got to die—while Brahman is eternal; and that Jones, as Jones, is other than Juarez, Jinnah, and all the rest of them—while Brahman within all of them is one. Jones, in his illusion of separateness, is tormented by feelings of envy, hate, or fear toward these seemingly separate beings around him. Or else he feels drawn to some of them by desire or love and is tormented because he cannot possess them and become one with them completely.

Separateness, says Vivekananda, is an illusion which can and must be dispelled through love of the eternal Brahman within ourselves and within all other beings. Therefore the practice of religion is a denial of separateness and a renunciation of its objectives: fame, wealth, power over others.

I—Mr. or Ms. Jones—am made uneasy by these statements. I work for my possessions and I don't want to give them up. I am proud to be Jones and would hate to be Jablochov; besides, I suspect him of planning to take my possessions away from me. And then I am not just any old Jones, I am *the* Jones, the famous one, so I am unwilling to think of myself as an all-pervading nonperson. I thoroughly approve of the word *love*. But, to me, "love" means Jane or John, and she or he is the most precious of all my possessions, whom I can only think of in exclusive relation to myself.

On the other hand, prudence advises me not to reject Vivekananda's teaching. My very uneasiness is an admission that what he says is at least partly true. I do get tense and depressed when I think about the future. My doctor has prescribed tranquilizers, but they don't make me tranquil, only dull and sleepy. So why not devote a few minutes a day to this meditation? It's a kind of insurance, really. I take out hospital insurance in the superstitious hope that it will save me from ever having to go into the hospital. Why not take out Vivekananda insurance in the hope that it will somehow save Jones from dying and losing his identity?

Good, says Vivekananda, with an indulgent smile. By all means make a start—even if it's for the wrong reason. He is endlessly good humored and patient. He never despairs of us because he knows—knows with the utter certainty of direct experience—that Brahman, our real nature, will gradually draw us to itself:

> So never mind these failures, these little backslidings. Hold the ideal a thousand times, and if you fail a thousand times, make the attempt once more. . . . There is infinite life before the soul. Take your time and you will achieve your end.

This sounds almost too reassuring, too soothing. Can he be making fun of us? No and yes. He means exactly what he says, but he is speaking in terms of the doctrine of reincarnation. When he says that we may take our time, he means that we are at liberty to remain in the bondage of ignorance for another thousand lifetimes; to go on dying and being reborn over and over again, until we have had enough of our separateness and have become seriously determined to end it. If we find Vivekananda's words reassuring—well, the joke is on us.

But what about *this* lifetime? Vivekananda once remarked:

> In trying to practice religion, eighty percent of people turn cheats

and about fifteen percent go mad; only the remaining five percent attain the immediate knowledge of the infinite Truth.

Does this shock you? If it does, imagine how you would react if you were told by the instructor at a gymnasium that "in trying to practice these exercises, eighty percent of my pupils cheat—by not doing the difficult exercises properly—and about fifteen percent overexercise like madmen until they injure themselves and have to quit; only the remaining five percent really transform their physique." Would you be surprised? Surely not, though you might well become depressed. You might decide, recognizing your own weakness, not to enroll at the gymnasium at all.

But there is no more miserable excuse for inaction than our claim to be weak, unspiritual, unworthy. When we make it, Vivekananda thunders at us that we are lions, not sheep; Brahman, not Jones. Then he turns gentle again and coaxes us to do something at least, to make some little effort, even if we are old, sick, burdened with dependents and worldly duties, hopelessly poor or hopelessly rich. He reminds us that true renunciation is mental, not necessarily physical. We are not required to disown our husbands or wives and turn our children out of doors. We must only try to realize that they are not really ours; to love them as dwelling places of Brahman, not as mere individuals. We must realize also that our so-called possessions are just toys which have been lent to us to play with for a little while. A string of beads can be pretty. So can a diamond necklace. There is no danger in wearing the necklace when we have stopped being aware of their difference in price.

Again and again, Vivekananda makes us laugh, as he begs us not to waste time repenting, not to moan and groan over our sins; bids us dry our tears and see the fun in this mock world which we have been taking so seriously. Thus, for a short while at least, he fills us with courage.

But Vivekananda did not devote all his tremendous energy

to prodding forward the fainthearted ninety-five percent. He needed helpers in his work—dedicated men and women on whom he could rely—and for these he did not search among the weak. From time to time, unexpectedly, in the middle of a lecture, he would make one of his thrilling, resounding appeals to the strong, the still uncorrupted five percent:

Men and women of today! If there be among you any pure, fresh flower, let it be laid on the altar of God. If there are among you any who, being young, do not desire to return into the world, let them give up! Let them renounce! This is the one secret of spirituality, renunciation. Dare to do this. Be brave enough to do it. Such great sacrifices are necessary.

Can you not see the tide of death and materialism that is rolling over these Western lands? Can you not see the power of lust and unholiness, that is eating into the very vitals of society? Believe me, you will not arrest these things by talk, or by movements of agitation for reform; but by renunciation, by standing up, in the midst of decay and death, as mountains of righteousness. Talk not, but let the power of purity, the power of chastity, the power of renunciation, emanate from every pore of your body. Let is strike those who are struggling day and night for gold, that even in the midst of such a state of things, there can be one to whom wealth counts for nothing. Put away lust and wealth. Sacrifice yourselves.

But who is it that will do this? Not the worn-out or the old, bruised and battered by society, but the Earth's freshest and best, the strong, the young, the beautiful. Lay down your lives. Make yourselves servants of humanity. Be living sermons. This, and not talk, is renunciation.

Do not criticise others, for all doctrines and all dogmas are good; but show them by your lives that religion is no matter of books and beliefs, but of spiritual realization. Only those who have seen it will understand this; but such spirituality can be given to others, even though they be unconscious of the gift. Only those who have attained to this power are amongst the great teachers of mankind. They are the powers of light.

The more of such men any country produces, the higher is that country raised. That land where no such men exist, is doomed. Nothing can save it. Therefore my Master's message to the world is, "Be ye all spiritual! Get ye first realization!"

You have talked of the love of man, till the thing is in danger of becoming words alone. The time is come to act. The call now is, Do! Leap into the breach, and save the world!

Once, in my own life, I have heard that challenge echoed, in the simplest possible way. A group had gathered to discuss religious matters. Several of those present spoke at length and with eloquence about God and the life of prayer. Then, when the last of them had finished, a fourteen-year-old boy exclaimed abruptly, with intense excitement: "But—if that's all true—why do we ever do anything else?"

The question left us silent.

VIVEKANANDA AND SARAH
BERNHARDT

In Paris, during the late summer of 1900, Swami Vivekananda had a conversation with the most famous woman of the Western world. It was probably, but not certainly, their first meeting. The two-volume *Life of Vivekananda,* by his Eastern and Western disciples, refers somewhat vaguely to an earlier occasion, in the United States, on which actress Sarah Bernhardt "sought an interview with him" (that hardly sounds like the imperious Sarah, who had made royalty take its hat off in her presence!) "and expressed her admiration and intense interest in the sublime teaching of the philosophy he so eloquently and truly represented." The date given for this encounter, 1895, would seem, in any case, to be wrong. Bernhardt was not in the States that year, though she visited them for a six-month tour in 1896. Moreover, Swamiji himself, writing in 1900 about the people he has met in Paris, particularly mentions that he and Madame Calvé, the singer, were previously acquainted, but speaks of Bernhardt as though they had just been introduced.

His correspondent was Swami Trigunatita, back home in India, and the tone of these travel letters, which were intended for publication, is instructive, gossipy, explosive, facetious, affectionate, and prophetic by turns; they are among the most characteristic things Vivekananda ever wrote. "Madame Bernhardt," he tells his brother monk, "is an aged lady; but when she steps on the stage after dressing, her imitation of the age and sex of the role she plays is perfect! A girl, or a boy,—whatever part you want her to play, she is an exact representation of that. And that wonderful voice! People here say, her voice has the ring of silver strings!"

In a couple of months, the "aged lady" was going to be fifty-six years old. Even the unkind camera shows us that, "on the stage after dressing," she did not look a day over thirty. Her photograph in the role of *L'Aiglon,* the Duke of Reichstadt, which she played for the first time in March of that year, presents an astonishingly slender and erect little personage in a riding coat and high boots with spurs, neither boy nor girl, woman nor man, sexless, ageless, and altogether impossible by daylight, outside the walls of a theater. Some later references in another of the letters to the story of Napoleon's tragic son suggest that Vivekananda must almost certainly have been Sarah in this, her greatest dramatic triumph after *La Dame aux Camélias.*

Bernhardt was then on the final peak of her mountainous career. Her acting was probably better than it had ever been before: better, certainly, than in the nineties, when her hit-or-miss noisiness, ranting, and hammering had provoked the brilliant scolding of the young theater critic Bernard Shaw, and his unfavorable comparisons between her and the more modern restraint of Eleonora Duse. She had disciplined herself, artistically and emotionally. The crazy days of her publicity—of the balloon trip, the coffin, and the shooting of the St. Louis Bay bridge—were far behind her. The shameful tragedy of her marriage with Damala had been ended, long ago, by his death from morphine poisoning. Her extravagance was still immense, but so were her earnings. And the accident in Rio de Janeiro which was to result in her gradual crippling was still five years ahead.

Swamiji seems to have been taken round to visit her in her dressing room at the theater after a performance. One wonders who introduced them, what word was used to describe the Swami's occupation to the actress, and whether she had already heard of him. "Madame Bernhardt," writes Vivekananda, "has a special regard for India; she tells me again and again that our country is *"très ancien, très civilisé"*—very ancient and very civilised." There must have been a gleam in Swamiji's eye as he politely received this flattering information.

They talked, as was natural, of the only play Sarah had ever produced with an Indian setting. It was *Izéil,* by Morand and Silvestre, an expensive flop. Bernhardt had always obstinately liked this piece, perhaps because it displayed her undoubted talent for theatrical décor. "She told me that for about a month she had visited every museum and made herself acquainted with the men and women, and their dress, the streets and bathing ghats and everything relating to India."

"Madame Bernhardt," the letter concludes, "has a very strong desire to visit India. *"C'est mon rêve*—It is the dream of my life," she says. Again, the Prince of Wales had promised to take her over to a tiger and elephant hunting excursion. But then she said, she must spend some two lacs of rupees if she went to India! She is of course in no want of money. *"La divine Sarah"*—the divine Sarah—is her name—how can she want money?—She who never travels but by a special train! That pomp and luxury many a prince of Europe cannot afford to indulge in! One can only secure a seat in her performance by paying double the fees, and that a month in advance! Well, she is not going to suffer want of money! But Sarah Bernhardt is given to spending lavishly. Her travel to India is therefore put off for the present."

Underneath these few mock-serious, bantering sentences, one senses the warmth of an immediate sympathy and liking. You can picture Swamiji sitting opposite the vivid, Semitic little Frenchwoman, large and jolly, his amused glance taking in the whole luxurious setting, the jewels, the mirrors, the silks, the cosmetics, the marvelous robes. Here, as in all women every-where, he saluted his own daughter, sister, mother: here, as always, he bowed to the eternal Godhead, beneath yet another of those queer disguises which bewilder our wanderings toward self-realization. Here, also, he surely recognized, to an unusual degree, the virtue he prized so highly: courage. Courage was, perhaps, the one quality which these fantastically dissimilar personalities had in common: the courage which had supported Vivekananda in the blackest hours of spiritual torment, of his master's loss, of all the early struggles and trials of the order, and which had never deserted him in the jungle or the mountains or the drawing rooms of American millionaires: the courage which had nerved Sarah in her battles to raise her child, in her work during the siege of Paris, in her defense of Dreyfus, in her return to the stage at the end of seventy-two after the amputation of her right leg. Swamiji must have been aware of this, and loved her for it.

And how did Bernhardt think of him? Perhaps, curiously enough, as a kind of colleague. Had not he, also, appeared triumphantly before the public? Many actors and actresses, including Sarah herself as Joan of Arc, have represented saints— at any rate, to the satisfaction of the audience beyond the footlights. Swamiji, on the other hand, with his superb presence and sonorous voice, might well have been mistaken for a great actor.

In a photograph of this period, we see how the eyes of the young sannyasin, burning almost intolerably with mingled devotion and doubt, have softened and deepened in the face of the mature man. The big lips and the line spreading from the wide nostrils, have a curve of watchful humor, in which there is either irony, nor bitterness, nor resignation—only a great calm, like the sea, with certainty dawning over it, an absolute, arising sun. "Are you never serious, Swamiji?" somebody asked him, rather reproachfully, and was answered: "Oh, yes. When I have the belly ache." Even this was an overstatement; for the smiling, joking Vivekananda of 1900 was already a very sick man.

He and Bernhardt never saw each other again. In October, the swami's party left Paris for Austria, the Balkans, and Egypt, whence he sailed to India, arriving home at the Belur monastery early in December. Thus ended his last journey to the West. The longer journey, also, was nearly over. One day in July 1902, wishing perhaps to spare his friends the agony of a goodbye, he passed, by stealth as it were, into *samadhi* and did not come back.

Sarah survived him for twenty-one years, survived the First World War, lived on into the era of Chaplin and Pickford and the Keystone Cops, appeared in two or three movies herself, and died in action, getting ready to rehearse a new play.

In the half dozen Bernhardt biographies I have been able to consult, the name of Vivekananda is not even mentioned. In fact, this brief anecdote of their meeting, with its exchange of conventional small talk and politeness, would seem to have no point whatsoever. That is just what makes it so fascinating and so significant. When poets or politicians foregather, we expect epigrams and aphorisms; for talk is their medium of expression. But talk is not, primarily, the medium of the man of illumination. His way of approach is more direct, more subtle, and more penetrating. He makes contact with you below the threshold of everyday awareness. No matter whether he speaks of the Prince of Wales, or of God, or only smiles and says nothing: your whole life will be, to some degree, changed from that moment on.

That is why—despite the biographers' silence, and the lack of high-class philosophical conversation—one dare not say that Swamiji's visit made no great or lasting impression upon Sarah. The spotlight of history which reveals a tiny area of surface action so brightly, cannot help us here. The blackness of our spiritual ignorance hides equally the inner life of the great actress and the unknown servant girl. All we can venture to say is this: "One day, the two human mysteries known to this world as Bernhardt and Vivekananda met, exchanged certain signals which we do not understand, and parted, we do not know why. All we *do* know is that their meeting, like every other event in this universe, did not take place by accident.

Swami Shivananda:
A Man of God

The story of Swami Shivananda is the story of a saint. A "natural" saint, one might call him. For, just as a few men in every age are born with a natural genius for science or the arts—a genius which manifests itself already in their earliest years—so also there are a few, a very few, who are born with spiritual genius. Swami Shivananda was one of those rare beings.

Mental conflict and struggle are, of course, inseparable from the practice of spiritual disciplines. The way to realization is always hard. Most men only achieve it after long periods of doubt and agony which are painful even when we merely read about them in a book. But when we read the life of a natural saint, a born spiritual genius, we can do so without pain, because the issue of his struggles seems certain even from the beginning. We know that he will win through.

Outwardly, Swami Shivananda led an intensely active life. As a young monk he traveled all over India. As an elderly man, he became the head of the Ramakrishna Order and was beset by the problems of a great and growing institution. Yet, inwardly, that life seems like a firm-set and abiding tower, based upon the rock of contemplation. The body wandered and wore itself out in service; the spirit remained calm and established. Very early it had found its timeless home, and there it always reposed.

When a great teacher, a Christ or a Ramakrishna, passes from the earth, he leaves behind him a group of followers who are determined to perpetuate the spirit of his teaching. Inevitably, this group forms itself into an order, a church, an organization. And here a danger arises. The teacher has proclaimed: "My kingdom is not of this world." But the church which embodies his teaching is a physical entity with members, buildings, funds, and a position in time and space. As it grows, it acquires potential political influence. And there will be many who will say that it should use its influence in human affairs, that it should intervene—with the aid of human weapons, if necessary—to protect and enlarge itself, here, in the physical world.

This deadly fallacy—which has cost the lives of millions throughout history, and which must lead, in the end, to the distortion and prostitution of the teacher's original message—was recognized and rejected by Swami Shivananda. Warmly as he sympathized with India's struggle for political liberation, deeply as he felt for the sufferings of her masses, he knew that spiritual power is a universal function or it is nothing. It cannot be diverted to serve local political purposes, however admirable. It cannot be used to achieve material objectives. To his eternal honor, Swami Shivananda refused to exert the influence of the Ramakrishna Order in the sphere of politics, despite his admiration for Gandhi's noncooperation movement. Gandhi had his own place and duty in the scheme of things, and he fulfilled it gloriously. But the man of contemplation, the vehicle of spiritual power, has another place and a different kind of duty. Swami Shivananda did not forget the words of the Gita: "The duty of another will bring you into great spiritual danger."

If you visit one of those huge dams which control the outflow of a lake or a river, you can go down into the engine room and see the turbines, supplying electricity to an entire countryside. It is very quiet down there. The turbines seem motionless and almost silent. And yet water is rushing through them at a hundred miles an hour—a terrific force which, if it were checked, would shatter the whole dam to pieces. The great saints are like that: calm, impersonal, holding back nothing for themselves, existing only to transmit the tremendous spiritual power which rushes through them and gives light to the surrounding world.

ON GIRISH GHOSH

Girish Ghosh was one of the great dramatists and poets of Bengal, India, and one of Ramakrishna's greatest devotees.

Since Girish lived primarily in the world, it's good to begin by reminding ourselves of the situation in Calcutta in the mid-nineteenth century in which he lived.

The following two extracts from the book *Ramakrishna and His Disciples* sketch something of the atmosphere between the British and the population of Calcutta at that time and the general clash of ideas that affected everybody in the city and country.

In those days, the city of Calcutta was the seat of British rule in India and the main port of entry for the ideas and culture of the West. The changes that were taking place in India, for the worse and for the better, all had their beginnings there.

The British had been peacefully established for more than seventy years. They had built an imposing European Quarter—"a city of palaces," one contemporary traveler called it; while another was reminded of St. John's Wood in London. Its architecture was predominantly neoclassical; the larger mansions had stately columns and massive porticoes, and their rooms were vast, airy, and scantily furnished in order to lessen the heat. Here, the social life was elegant and excessively formal. The high British officials rode around town in carriages with outriders; on their arrival at evening parties, servants would run ahead of them carrying flaming torches. Their families went to church and to the opera, their ladies drove out along the Esplanade and gossiped about each other, their sons played cricket. Despite the climate, everything was done to preserve the atmosphere of home. As for the Bengalis, they usually saw the insides of these palatial homes only in the capacity of servants. And even when some wealthy high-caste families were occasionally invited to receptions, it was scarcely on a basis of friendly equality. Only recently, British Calcutta society had been plunged into controversy because Lord Auckland the Governor-General had actually permitted forty-five Bengali college boys to appear in his presence wearing shoes! As the century advanced, however, many of these barriers were gradually broken down.

The British in India at that period must have seemed strange, paradoxical beings to any detached observer. They were imperialists with bad consciences. They were builders of bridges, roads, hospitals, and schools—public benefactors who were nevertheless ceaselessly engaged in the piecemeal conquest of a nation. For the Indians, who did not want them, they sacrificed their health and their lives, going back to England prematurely aged, yellow-faced, on crutches, to die. Tens of thousands of them were buried in the country during the two centuries of their occupation. Many were altruistic, many were heroic, many were deeply devout and felt that they had accepted voluntary exile in this savage and unhealthy land in order to do God's work among the benighted. What almost none of them seem to have been aware of was that they were in the most religious country in the world; and in the presence of a spiritual culture which made their own sectarianism seem provincial indeed. Even Honoria Lawrence, wife of Sir Henry Lawrence, certainly one of the noblest and most dedicated Englishwomen in India, could write coldly: "There is something very oppressive in being surrounded by heathen and Mohammedan darkness, in seeing idol-worship all around, and when we see the deep and debasing hold these principles have on the people, it is difficult to believe they can ever be freed from it."*

One of the many evils of foreign conquest is the tendency of the conquered to imitate their conquerors. This kind of imitation is evil because it is uncritical; it does not choose certain aspects of the alien culture and reject others, but accepts everything slavishly, with a superstitious belief that if you ape your conquerors you will acquire their superior power.

The British certainly had much to offer India that was valuable:

---

*Christopher Isherwood, *Ramakrishna and His Disciples* (Hollywood: Vedanta Press, 1965), 38–39.

medical science and engineering, the arts of the West, a clearly defined legal code. Unfortunately, they brought with them also two creeds—scientific atheism and missionary evangelism—diametrically opposed to each other yet equally narrow and dogmatic. These two creeds had done quite enough harm already in the West, where they were indigenous; exported to India, they had the added power of novelty and threatened to produce spiritual and cultural chaos. The young Indians who came into contact with them nearly all reacted violently. Either they lost belief in everything Hindu and got nothing from England in return but despair; or they were thrilled by the fanaticism and self-assurance of the missionaries and embraced a wretched version of Christianity which was both abject and self-seeking. (Since the missionaries had charge of most of the new educational facilities provided by the British, they got the opportunity to indoctrinate many of the most intelligent students of each generation.) Thus the young were growing up into cultural hybrids; laughed at and despised by the British because of their hopelessly silly efforts at imitation; condemned by orthodox Hindus of the old school as impious traitors to the religion and traditions of their race.**

All of this is described because what has to be said about Girish Ghosh has a great deal to do with the concept of sin, which shall be covered shortly. First, a little background on Girish's life:

Girish Chandra Ghosh was born in 1844 in Calcutta in the district of Baghbazar. His parents both died while he was young. He was married soon afterwards, but the marriage did not stabilize his life.

Girish was a person of great animal vitality, strength, ingenuity, force, drive, and, indeed, genius. A protean kind of talent, he was a poet, dramatist, also an actor, and he threw himself into everything with the utmost vitality. It was an aspect or function of this vitality that he was also exceedingly sensual, had a considerable sex life that was much discussed by

---

**Ramakrishna and His Disciples*, 154–155.

everybody concerned around him, and he drank alcohol in enormous quantities and took opium, etc.

A modern poet has said that a saint is easy to recognize: his constitution is designed for vice. By this he meant, in the case of a person like Girish, that without this energy he would not have had all the positive qualities as well as the negative ones. His early life was a succession of boring office jobs that were quickly abandoned. Meanwhile, his spare time was divided between writing and amateur acting. He was very fond of practical jokes. I think personally that people who play practical jokes are fundamentally very aggressive, and this aggression appeared in various forms later in his life.

Girish was the type of person fairly common already in nineteenth-century Europe as a bohemian artist, but he wasn't such a familiar type in Calcutta since standards of Hinduism on the one hand and the standards of missionary Christianity on other had long had a tremendous hold on people's feelings. There was a great deal of puritanism which judged him to be a debauched man.

This is all the negative side of his character. On the positive side, he was enormously productive. He revived the dramatic life of Bengal, literally from the dead. He began to write plays that were both devotional in the most classic sense and written in a sort of Shakespearean style. He wrote both historical plays and contemporary plays of the nineteenth century which were written in a Bengali colloquial style.

In these plays, he often played not only one but several parts, and before long, while in his thirties and forties, he acquired a theater, called the Star Theater (which exists to this day in Calcutta). In the theater, he was constantly putting on the new plays he had written. Such was the situation at the time when he met Ramakrishna.

His meetings with Ramakrishna were interesting because Girish was really a devotional person who had been looking all these years for someone to help him. Throughout his early life he was not easily taken in. He was very loath to accept any human whatsoever as a guru, much less to accept any seeming human being as an avatar.

Girish, in an article which he wrote later in life, described his state of mind before he met Ramakrishna:

> In a crisis I thought: "Does God exist? Does he listen to the prayers of man? Does he show the way from darkness to light?"
>
> My mind said yes. Immediately I closed my eyes and prayed: "Oh God, if you exist, carry me. Give me refuge; I have none."
>
> But I had nurtured doubt all these years. I had argued long saying that there was no God. And again, I fell victim to doubt, for I had not the courage to say boldly that God does not exist.

There you see a mirror image in a Bengali mind of what was previously described as the influence of the scientific atheism imported on the one hand from the West and of the vigorous Christian missionary puritanism. He alternated. What he had, as a matter of fact, was a native spiritual vigor which far exceeded anything offered by the missionaries of the conquering nation.

> Everyone to whom I discussed my problem said unanimously that without instruction from a guru, doubt would not go and nothing could be achieved in spiritual life. But my intellect refused to accept a human being as a guru.

The first time Girish saw Ramakrishna was at the home of an attorney who lived in his neighborhood. He'd heard that this Paramahamsa (great holy man) existed. (This happened around 1880 when Ramakrishna was in his middle years.)

He went to the house and Ramakrishna was sitting there in a high spiritual state and seemed almost unaware of his surroundings. Lamps were lighted—it was in the evening—and Ramakrishna looked around and said, "Is it evening?" and Girish thought, "What a fake! He's putting on airs."

Girish, it should be noted, was a very good tester in one way, because like all actors, he deeply suspected all behavior at its surface level, and would look at any behavior to see what was underneath and what it was all about. I think that actors come to feel, just because they play different roles, a sort of instinctive sense of the unreality of the surface personality of anybody. What I mean is that they're always thinking, "Well, yes, that's all very well, but you know, one can switch at any moment. What does it mean? What guarantee is there that this man is on the level?"

Several years later, Girish again saw Ramakrishna. This time he was much more favorably impressed, largely because Ramakrishna, instead of sitting in utter meditative grandeur and ignoring everybody and expecting to be bowed down to (according to the Indian custom), was the very reverse. Every time he met somebody he bowed down to them. This delighted Girish because it was so out of character and not the conventional role of an Indian holy man.

Of course, in India, one could easily see so-called holy men in large numbers, and this only added to Girish's skepticism.

And then, on September 21, 1884, Ramakrishna and some of the devotees visited the Star Theater to see Girish's devotional play about the life of the great Indian saint Sri Chaitanya. One of the devotees came to Girish and said that Ramakrishna had come to see the play and it would be very kind if he would give him a free pass. If not, then one of the devotees would pay for his ticket. Girish said that Ramakrishna need not pay, but the others would have to.

Girish was still the actor/manager. He wasn't overly impressed yet by Ramakrishna. I think he was frightened. That is what seems to come out when you see the whole of his life. He felt himself on the verge of some extremely disturbing and life-shaking experience, and he was on the defensive.

Then a rather ridiculous scene took place. Girish went out to greet Ramakrishna and was about to bow down, when Ramakrishna bowed down to him. So he bowed down to Ramakrishna, and Ramakrishna bowed right back. This went on several times until at last Girish realized that he had to stop it, so he only bowed down mentally. After that, Ramakrishna went to his seat with the others.

Ramakrishna was very impressed by the play, which must have pleased Girish immensely. Indeed, Ramakrishna remarked, "I found the representation the same as the reality."

Of course, these kinds of remarks mean very little as a rule, but if you can imagine Ramakrishna saying that with the authority of knowing what the reality was, then you can imagine that this was about the greatest compliment he could possibly pay anybody. It takes a little imagination to think yourself in his position, because Girish must have been aware by this time that he was in the presence of a very strange and extraordinary individual.

Then, again they met, this time in someone's home. By now Girish was taken by the idea of wanting a guru, and thinking about what a guru should be like. "What is a guru?" he said. Ramakrishna replied, "He's like a matchmaker. A matchmaker arranges for the union of the bride with the bridegroom. Likewise, a guru prepares for the meeting of the individual soul and his beloved, the divine spirit." (Actually, he did not use the word *matchmaker,* but a slang expression more forceful, like procurer. It's so typical of Ramakrishna that he always used words that related to a person's life style.) And then Ramakrishna added, "But you don't have to worry about the guru. Yours has already been chosen."

It was a tremendous moment for Girish.

Then they began to talk about the theater. Girish became embarrassed when Ramakrishna again praised the play and said how remarkable it was. So Girish responded by becoming rude and aggressive. He said, "I don't know anything about that. I don't care about the play or Chaitanya. I just wrote it to make money."

Ramakrishna ignored this. Then he said to Girish, "Whatever you say, you do know something. There is something in you that recognizes the godlike. It is only when you can recognize the godlike that you can write about it."

Girish said, "Well, after all, it's nothing. I think I should give it up. It's silly, all this scribbling."

But Ramakrishna said, "No! Absolutely not! You should go on writing. That should be your work. You do a great deal of good by it."

So now we can see the curious duel, which Ramakrishna had with almost all of his disciples, especially with Swami Vivekanada: the duel between the forces of the other person, which were resisting, and with Ramakrishna's open and pure love, his invitation to come to him. And this took various forms.

The thing that strikes one when reading about Girish is that really, he and Ramakrishna were in a curious way very much alike. They were both children of Bengal, very volatile and vivacious. They were born actors with a strong love of dance and music.

When I was taken to the Star Theater by Swami Prabhavananda in 1963, there was a play in Bengali, a modern play. I didn't understand a word, but I didn't want to leave. I would have sat there for hours. It was the power of these people, the actors. There was something in their style of acting, in the enormous gusto, their facial expressions, their gestures, the sense that something simply terrific was going on.

The story was actually a domestic farce, but you felt that this could be applied to anything, in the enormous gusto of the performance. It was something I could never tire of watching. And you can glimpse there something of the extraordinary Bengali temperament, which both Ramakrishna and Girish had.

There were the famous scenes, often quoted, where Girish took to visiting Ramakrishna very late at night while drunk. Girish was very fond of having tremendous longing for Ramakrishna when he was visiting his various girlfriends, etc. He would rush out to get a cab and say he had to see Ramakrishna.

He arrived—nothing could be more tiresome—in the middle of the night. And—this was so characteristic—Ramakrishna welcomed him completely. And then they would dance.

I think there's a great significance in this dancing. We hear again and again of how Ramakrishna would see drunks in the road while traveling who were perfect strangers, and how he would get out the carriage and dance with them. This gives us an insight into the nature of so-called sin, or whatever you call getting drunk.

In other words, what Ramakrishna profoundly understood and taught to us was that all our so-called vices are in fact frustrated attempts to find the truth, or to find peace, or to find release from something. For example, you may be frightened, feel menaced, and see enemies everywhere, so you give the orders, and a million people are killed. Or again on a smaller scale, you know you want to shut out reality because it seems threatening and alarming. You long for some other kind of truth. You long for some kind of transcendental thing, and you therefore proceed to take some drug or other; not to be wicked or vicious, but because you want to find a release, a higher inner truth.

Of course, nowadays we're much more sophisticated than we used to be about these things, and people do understand that, I think, to a greater extent. I think we all do. But you see, that is why Ramakrishna, looking at a drunkard dancing, could think that this is exactly the same as ecstacy. It's only that the drunk is going about it the wrong way. Ramakrishna saw the drive behind it, the desire for something that is a state of joy, of joy in the Eternal. Therefore he felt a tremendous kinship with people who were in this condition.

There was one time when Girish did one of his midnight descents on Ramakrishna and suddenly said, "Where's my bottle? I haven't got a bottle!" Ramakrishna said, "That's quite all right." And it turned out that before Girish's carriage had left, Ramakrishna had sent one of his disciples particularly to collect

Girish's bottle from the carriage. When it was brought in, he said, "Go ahead, drink some more."

Girish said, "I couldn't do that here, you know."

Ramakrishna said, "Nonsense. Go on, make the most of it. Drink it while you want to. You'll give up drinking one of these days."

So Girish drank right in front of Ramakrishna. You see how Ramakrishna broke down the conventional puritanism, the outside layer, and thus broke down the standards of mere respectability and its opposite, which we impose on everything. Everybody, in a way, who isn't respectable is in a kind of minor state of grace in relation to people who are respectable, simply because there's a truth to it. Even in the disgrace there's a sort of truth. You find this in the characters of Russian novels who are always getting drunk or whatever and then repenting, as in the great masterpieces of the nineteenth century such as *The Brothers Karamazov.*

Ramakrishna himself would be unconventional and scandalous in other ways. Girish gave him one time what was a marvelous compliment. He said, "Everything about you is illegal." What he meant was that Ramakrishna broke all the laws of orthodox Hinduism.

There is the well-known scene when a cat came into the shrine while Ramakrishna was performing the worship. Ramakrishna realized suddenly that the Eternal was also in the cat. He was about to offer food to the deity when he bowed down instead before the cat and gave the cat the food. People were absolutely horrified by what he did. Ramakrishna was nearly thrown out of his job as the temple priest, although he had just given the supreme illustration of what Vedanta is all about.

Ramakrishna's demonstrations were invariably shocking, just because they were so graphic, so literal. It has to be said that the great spiritual figures in other religions had done the same sort of thing. One example that comes to mind is of the great

Christian St. Philip Neri, who took the injunction "suffer the little children to come unto me" quite literally. He let the children play on the high altar where they constantly were knocking over the sacred vessels. But he said their play was much more important. Many saw this, of course, so there were many complaints. People were jolted by this behavior.

The danger of not being respectable is that you have to boast about it. Girish was indeed tiresome about this. He said how, if you could see all the bottles of wine he had drunk, it would be as high as Mt. Everest. (In India, it is a terrible thing to drink alcohol.) This was all very well, but it didn't prove anything except that he had accepted the miserable puritanical standards instead of looking at them the way Ramakrishna did, and as he gradually learned to.

The whole point of the life of Girish is that he came right through this. It was not so much to some kind of improvement in behavior, although that followed, nor to becoming a good boy, or anything of that sort. But he developed a deep devotion to Sri Ramakrishna, about which Swami Vivekananda said, "Nobody has devoted himself or abandoned his will so absolutely to that of the Master as has Girish."

Girish once asked for instructions from Sri Ramakrishna, and said, "What shall I do?"

Ramakrishna replied, "Try calling on God three times a day."

Girish said, "I'm sorry, I can't promise to. I might forget."

"Well, do it twice. Do it once."

"No, no, I can't promise anything."

"All right," said Sri Ramakrishna. "Give me your power of attorney. I'll take it over and be responsible for you. Now, you have no will at all. You will only say, 'I'll do whatever the Lord wills.' Don't ever say again, 'I will do this. I will not do that.' "

And Girish really began to live in this spirit. This is something with which we, at such a distance in time, can only take the word of observers. But it does seem that Girish did turn into the devotee that is really a saint. He had thrown himself at Sri Ramakrishna's feet. That was the way he lived.

Girish outlived Sri Ramakrishna by many years and died at the age of 68 in 1912. He left a tremendous tradition.

When one thinks about him, one comes back to that tremendous line in the Gita:

> The Lord is everywhere
> And always perfect;
> What does he care for man's sin
> Or the righteousness of man.

PART IV

THE WRITER AND VEDANTA

The Writer and Vedanta

The question is whether we can find some relationship between Vedanta philosophy and the practice of an art. I shall speak specifically about the art of fiction, of writing novels and stories, but as you will see, some of my remarks will apply equally to the arts of music, painting, drawing, and sculpture.

The two propositions of Vedanta which we have to consider are these: Vedanta says that a Reality exists beneath all the outer layers—the external appearances—of this universe; a Reality, or, to use a word more related to the Christian tradition, a Godhead. This reality, or Godhead, is called in the Sanskrit language Brahman. And when this Godhead is thought of, not as all-surrounding but as within the individual—and of course it is simultaneously both—then Brahman is called the Atman. But Brahman-Atman are one and the same and these two words simply express its two relationships to the individual.

The second proposition of Vedanta which concerns us here is that the aim of life is to make contact with and unitively know this Godhead, this Atman, within one's self, and by knowing it within one's self, to be able to know it everywhere; to know the Atman as Atman, and then to understand thereby that the Atman is Brahman.

Very well. Now what is the art of writing? It seems to me that the purpose of the art of writing is to understand, to reveal the deeper nature of experience, to make life and its phenomena, and all the human beings and creatures around us more significant. To make our own lives fuller of meaning and thereby to render our whole experience moment by moment more significant than it otherwise would be. To open our eyes, to open our ears, and above all to open our hearts to the experience around us.

In the course of history the arts have often been attacked by those who have felt that they lead only to preoccupation with this world and its beauties, and that they thereby deflect the mind from what is eternal. It has been said therefore that the arts are dangerous, that they lead to sensuousness, to sensuality, to preoccupation with the surface of life, and a forgetfulness of its inwardness.

There is another extreme attitude which is very prevalent nowadays, and that is to regard art as a substitute for religion. This attitude toward art is, I think, as mistaken as the other; and it is a by-product of what has been called Sunday religion. Just as there is Sunday religion, there is also Sunday art. Sunday religion is the religion of people who want to go into some suitable building once a week, and feel nice and reverent and uplifted before lunch. Such people can quite easily pass from the use of a church or a temple or a synagogue to going into an art gallery, let us say, and feeling nice and reverent and uplifted by art before lunch. Such Sunday art, such banishment of art into a kind of shrine where it is isolated from everyday life, is every bit as pernicious as the banishment of religion into a shrine where it is isolated from our daily life. And people who thus isolate either religion or art or both, can usually be known by their attitude to those who seriously practice either religion or art. The people who like Sunday art wish very much that you could do without those horrid creatures the artists, because while the art is so beautiful and is safe inside a gallery or in the hundred best books or a nice concert hall, these dreadful artists have deplorable habits and are noisy and loud and obstreperous and antisocial and cause scandals. In just the same manner—not that I am suggesting a direct comparison between them—the people who have seriously practiced religion and achieved the greatest spiritual insight have often been very strange characters from the point of view of the Sunday religionists. Many of the saints have caused infinite scandal to the merely pious, by their odd, unconventional, bohemian, and even seemingly blasphemous behavior, simply because they were approaching the Reality with total belief. The life of Sri Ramakrishna is full of instances in which he caused great shock and offense, not to unbelievers, but to people who by their own lights were very pious and devout.

But now to come back to the question of the relation between Vedanta and practice of the art of writing. Vedanta philosophy describes what it calls yogas. It means any way of life, any approach which will lead us toward union with God. There are several clearly recognized paths, several different yogas.

One generally thinks of karma yoga in terms of feeding the hungry or caring medically for the sick or working on projects such as those in which the Quakers of the Society of Friends constantly engage, building schools or laying out new villages in some impoverished area. What I am going to suggest to you is that perhaps the practice of the arts may also under certain circumstances claim to be regarded as a form of karma yoga.

In support of this suggestion, I'll first of all quote the pronouncement about karma yoga which is found in the Bhagavad Gita. Sri Krishna says: "You have the right to work, but for the work's sake only. You have no right to the fruits of work." In other words, you must do your duty, whatever it is— the kind of work which nature seems to have fitted you for— and then you must offer up the results of this work as a form of devotion, a form of sacrifice. You must do your work to the utmost extent of your powers, but you must not mind whether it fails, whether it succeeds, whether you are praised for it or blamed for it. That is only secondary, and in the last analysis, immaterial. If you do your work in this spirit then you are a karma yogin.

Now it seems clear that the best, the most dedicated of the

artists have in fact gone this far—that they have achieved a kind of dedication in which they have really worked for the work's sake only. They have been superior to the attraction of money and fame. They have not feared to speak the truth. They have been expelled from their countries, or arrested, or even lost their lives in this pursuit of the truth which is their duty and their way of self-dedication. One thinks, for example, of Zola, who did not fear to declare the innocence of Dreyfus. One thinks of Thomas Mann, who refused to remain in Germany under the Nazi regime and to be celebrated there as a great author, choosing instead to go into exile and to speak out against the lies which he detected in the Nazi propaganda.

Karma yoga, as we have seen, is fundamentally concerned with our fellow human beings. We try to serve the Atman within these fellow human beings. Writing also is concerned with human beings and the greatness of any individual writer depends to a large extent on the degree of compassion which he can feel toward human beings. By compassion I don't mean sentimentality or just pity, I mean a much larger kind of interest and love. This compassion is, of course, also very frequently demonstrated by dedicated scientists, and the zoologist who is studying the habits of the rattlesnake is not in the least sentimental about the rattlesnake. He doesn't suppose that it won't bite him if he makes a quick movement which startles it, but on the other hand, he does study it with an interest amounting to love.

Just as it's the privilege of the scientist to study absolutely anything, so there can be no question that the writer is privileged to write about absolutely anything. Any idea that there are suitable and unsuitable subjects for art is a sheer reactionary nonsense. What we have to ask ourselves is this: what is the *approach* of the writer to his subject? The subject in itself is not the question at issue. The writer may choose any character, any kind of situation; it's all a question of approach and treatment. The writer can write about any kind of evildoing, provided that he approaches it with compassion and without sentimentality. His compassion will consist in showing that evildoing is, in every case, a desperate, misguided attempt on the part of the evildoer to become free or happy. Why does one kill five million people? Simply because one is afraid of them and believes that one will be safer when they are dead. The most atrocious crimes are committed, in fact, with a misguided desire to achieve some kind of peace. And the writer must understand such problems and must be able to make others understand them.

The position of the writer in relation to his material can perhaps be shown by an analogy with Vedanta. Vedanta says that the reality is Brahman, Atman. Brahman has no attributes. Brahman does not act. Brahman is. Brahman is existence and consciousness. It is the power of Brahman which acts, and therefore the Vedantist has a concept which he calls Ishwara. Ishwara is Brahman united with its power. And you might say roughly that Ishwara is somewhat the same as the idea of God the Father in the Christian tradition. Ishwara has attributes and Ishwara is within the universe. Brahman projects the universe and all its appearances, and these are known as Maya. When Ishwara is incarnated in human form—the Vedantists believe he has been incarnated many times in the course of human history and will be incarnated many times in the future—then Ishwara *seems* to enter into the world. He seems to take part in action, he seems to be angry, he seems to be happy, he seems to be sad, he seems to say this is good, and this is evil; and yet according to the belief of Vedanta, he is, in fact, not involved in this Maya—he is always its master.

You have probably already seen the direction in which I am aiming. I am suggesting that this is also the position of a novelist within his novel. This is particularly true of novels in which the story is told in the first person singular, so that the novelist appears as one of his own characters, even if he is given another name. But most authors tend to put themselves to some extent into their books. One may then say that the author has incarnated himself among his characters. He shares in their struggles, he shares in their passions, he is apparently one of them. And yet, since he has created the entire situation himself, he is also master of his maya. He is not only within his world but also simultaneously looking down upon it and sanctioning it. He can say, as though he were Ishwara, "These are all my children, they all belong to me. I accept the good with the bad." A novelist may write about good characters and bad characters and seem to judge them, from one standpoint. And yet at the same time one is always aware that a great writer loves all his characters, and enjoys the badness of the bad just as much as the goodness of the good. Indeed, of course, the two are absolutely necessary to each other—for how can you exhibit the badness of the bad without having good characters; and how can you exhibit the goodness of the good without having bad characters? They all belong together, and they are all part of a universe over which the novelist presides. But of course the novelist is not Ishwara and the novel is not the universe. It's only a kind of tiny working model of something unimaginably greater.

Aldous Huxley made a marvelous speech once in my hearing, a speech which unfortunately has never been printed in his essays, but of which, luckily, I took a few notes. In this speech, he likened art to a net—a net which is cast out into experience, with the object of catching something. Yet, said Huxley, what really matters, paradoxically enough, is not the net itself but the holes in the net. He said, for example, that in a sense great music exists for the sake of its pauses; for instance, the pauses that occur in the middle of a Beethoven symphony. These pauses are of course quite unlike bits of ordinary silence, because the whole symphony has led up to them—they are held and defined, and the music goes on on the other side of them. Such pauses are silence charged with meaning. In the same way, in the art of scuplture, the gaps between the groups of statuary are not just gaps, but areas of emptiness which are defined by something else. In poetry again we have pauses of tremendous power, where a beat in the rhythm has been deliberately missed in order to create a kind of catch in the breath. Now as Huxley suggested, these apertures, these holes in the net, are really entrances to a world of spiritual knowledge which lies beyond the realm of sense knowledge. So we may say that, where art leaves off, religion begins, and that, from this point of view, the aim of art is to transcend art. Music transcends music by producing charged silence. Sculpture and painting transcend themselves by producing a charged nonrepresentational space. And I think that it is really only in this sense that one can talk about the relation between art and religious experience.

If one is a writer and has been involved in any kind of philosophy or religious belief, one is of course often asked: "Has this affected your writing?" I am very often asked: "In what way have you been influenced by Vedanta?" Well, there are various answers to this question. In the first place, certain concepts of Vedanta are very useful in the practice of any art. Vedanta cosmology teaches us that there are three forces called the gunas. And these three forces in different combinations make up the material world and also the underlying subtle world—the world which exists, as it were, below the outer skin of matter. The three gunas are said to be sattva, rajas, and tamas. Sattva is that which is radiant, shining, calm, illuminating. Rajas is that which is energetic, powerful, angry, destructively violent. Tamas is that which is inert, slothful, resistant, and at rest. Now to accept this hypothesis of the interacting gunas is, I think, psychologically very helpful to anybody who works in the arts.

Most writers—and no doubt most other artists—suffer from what is called "writer's block." Writer's block is what you feel on those terrible days when you simply cannot get started with any work—you feel a complete disinclination to do so. Now, in relation to the gunas, the condition of suffering from writer's block would be described as being in a state of tamas, with rajas absent, and sattva very dim. The Gita has something valuable to teach us about this. It says that the enlightened man does not hate any of the gunas. He does not even hate tamas. He sits apart from the gunas and regards their workings objectively. He waits until tamas has passed and a state of rajas has taken control; then he goes on with his work. I have been much comforted by this passage, and instead of becoming frantic when I feel under the influence of tamas, I say to myself that after all I must not hate even tamas while it prevails but must be ready immediately to work when rajas is ready to demonstrate itself. This is, of course, a dangerous doctrine, because it may be just an excuse for loitering. But it teaches us, I think, not to get unduly frantic if we do less work one day than another.

Again, of course, contact with Vedanta has made me see that of all characters, the saint is the most interesting. He is the most interesting because he is the most flexible and he is the most flexible because he is not driven by hate, fear, greed, and all the other limiting motives. He acts according to quite other principles and he can constantly astound us. Very few people have succeeded in writing well about saints in fiction just because it is so extraordinarily difficult. One of the best examples of this kind of flexible and therefore astounding behavior of a saint is the extraordinary scene in *The Brothers Karamazov*, when Father Zossima suddenly bows down to the earth in front of Dmitri Karamazov because he realizes what Dmitri doesn't yet know—the terrible future that is in store for him. Zossima bows down before him with the utmost compassion, and with a sense that he must share in the sorrows and sins of every other human being.

But, by and large, I must say that I think that the portrayal of saints in fiction is quite beyond the power of most of us, and therefore it's much more satisfactory to write about them in terms of biography. I have often thought this since I have been working on the biography of Ramakrishna. It would seem unwise to try to render this material in fictional form because, of course, the moment you have an imaginary figure, and the moment you have to invent fictional circumstances, then you have much greater difficulty in convincing the reader that all this could possibly have happened.

So, to conclude with a rather trite observation, I personally do not feel that Vedanta philosophy, any more than a political philosophy, is a fit subject for direct presentation in a work of fiction. When you try to put philosophical ideas into fiction the ideas stick out, and what results is a poorly disguised sermon. I think, in other words, that if you want to present the ideas of Vedanta philosophy, you should write an essay or a book which is explicitly about that philosophy.

THE PROBLEM OF THE
RELIGIOUS NOVEL

I suppose that most novelists have considered, at one time or another, the project of writing a religious novel. Every writer of dramatic fiction, irrespective of his individual beliefs or doubts, is eager to find characters who will exhibit the maximum variety of reactions to external events. The saint is preeminently such a character. Because his motives are not dictated by fear, vanity, or desire—because his every action is a genuine act of free will—you never can predict what he will do next. He accepts life more fully, more creatively, than any of his neighbors. And therefore he is the most interesting person to write about.

The most interesting and the most difficult. For, in attempting to present such a character to his audience of average men and women, the writer cannot rely at all on that factor of familiarity, of self-recognition, which assists him so powerfully when he is describing average people, recognizable social types. He cannot expect his audience to come halfway to meet him, exclaiming, "Why, that's just like Mr. Jones!" The saint, considered as an end product, resembles Mr. Jones as little as he resembles a giraffe. And yet Mr. Jones and Mr. Smith and Mr. Brown are all potentially saints. This is what the author has somehow to prove to his audience.

It is a task which demands the utmost persuasiveness, deftness, and cunning. At every step, prejudices and preconceptions have to be overcome. The public has its preconceived notion of a saint—a figure with a lean face and an air of weary patience, who alternates between moods of forbidding austerity and heartbroken sweetness—a creature set apart from this bad world, a living reproach to our human weakness, in whose presence we feel ill at ease, inferior, and embarrassed. In other words, the dreariest of bores.

If I ever write a religious novel, I shall begin by trying to prove that my saint-to-be really *is* Mr. Jones. Somerset Maugham, for example, does this quite successfully in *The Razor's Edge*. Larry, when we first meet him, is an entirely reassuring character, lively, natural, normal, a typical American boy. I think that Maugham's choice of such a character had a great deal to do with the immense popularity of his book.

So far, so good. But now a second and much greater problem arises. How am I going to show, in terms of dramatic fiction, that decisive moment at which my hero becomes aware of his vocation and decides to do something about it? Maugham is rather vague at this point: he merely suggests that Larry's change of heart is caused by his experiences in the First World War. Aldous Huxley's *Time Must Have a Stop* avoids the moment altogether—making a huge jump from Sebastian the precocious, cowardly, inhibited schoolboy to Sebastian the mature, meditative man, already far advanced in the practice of spiritual discrimination. One of the classic examples of a conversion scene is, of course, Dostoevski's account of the duel, in *The Brothers Karamazov*, which starts the process of turning a stupid young bully of a Russian officer into Father Zossima, the saint. How beautifully Dostoevski handles this moment of transformation—without the least sentimentality, in terms almost of farce, yet with such warmth, insight, and naturalness! We share the young man's exquisite relief when he finds himself suddenly able, by fearlessly asking his opponent's pardon, to break the bonds of a rigid military code which has hitherto conditioned his behavior, and to perform his first act of pure free will. This is the kind of scene I should like to have in my novel—something slightly comic and entirely natural. In history, we know that many conversions have occurred as the result of a vision. But visions, unless you are writing historical fiction, like *The Song of Bernadette,* seem to me to be undesirable in the early stages of a story, because they excuse the author from explaining what is happening in his hero's mind. Dramatically, they are a form of cheating.

It is all very well to use words like *conversion* in an article for a religious magazine. They belong to an accepted terminology. I know that my readers will understand what I mean. But this kind of shorthand is never permissible for the novelist, with his mixed and highly skeptical audience. He has to explain, as though they had never been explained before, his hero's motives and objectives, and this, in a religious novel, is particularly difficult. How am I to prove that X isn't merely insane when he turns his back on the whole scheme of pleasures, rewards, and satisfactions which are accepted by the Joneses, the Smiths, and the Browns, and goes in search of superconscious, extra-phenomenal experience? The only way I can see how to do this is with the help of the Joneses themselves. I must show that the average men and women of this world are searching, however unconsciously, for that same fundamental reality of which X has already had a glimpse. Certainly, they look for it in the wrong places. Certainly, their methods are quite unpractical. Mr. Jones will find nothing at the bottom of the whisky bottle except a headache. But the whisky bottle is not to be dismissed with a puritanical sneer; it is the crude symbol of Jones's dissatisfaction with surface consciousness, his need to look more deeply into the meaning of life. The Smiths conform obediently to the standards imposed by the advertisements they read in their newspapers. They drive the prescribed make of car, smoke the recommended brand of cigarettes, spend their leisure time in the ways and at the places which are guaranteed as educational and enjoyable—and yet, at the back of their minds, there is a germ of doubt. Is this really what we were born for? Is this the whole meaning of existence? That doubt may, one day, be their salvation. It is the measure of their kinship with X. For the evolving saint does not differ from his fellow humans in kind, but only in degree. That is why X can only be understood, artistically, when his story is related to that of the Joneses, the Smiths, and the Browns.

The greater part of my novel would deal, of course, with X's struggles toward sainthood, toward complete spiritual realization. I think that most writers have erred in making this phase of their story too somber and depressing. True, the path of the spiritual aspirant is hard. The mortification of the ego is tedious and painful. But I see no reason for the author to sentimentalize his hero's sufferings or to allow him to indulge in self-pity. Sportswriters find no pathos in the hardships of a boxer's training. The would-be saint is the last person in the world we should feel sorry for. His sufferings are purely voluntary. If his will slackens, they automatically cease. *The Garden of Allah** is not really a tragedy, unless one regards it as a tragedy of weakness. If the runaway monk did not genuinely want to return to the monastery, and was only bowing to public opinion, then it was very weak and silly of him to do so. George Moore, in his two movels, *Evelyn Innes* and *Sister Teresa,* has traced the development of a famous opera singer into a Catholic nun. It is a wonderful and moving story, full of acute psychological observation, amounting almost to clairvoyance. Moore is at his best in describing that moment of spiritual vertigo and despair when Evelyn, listening to the trivial chatter of the other novices, thinks, "How can I possibly stay here?" and then, remembering the equally trivial chatter at the dinner parties she used to attend, asks herself, "But how could I possibly go back to the old life?" Nevertheless, I feel that Moore, like many of his inferiors, has made his protagonist's spiritual history too gloomy—perhaps simply because he does not carry it far enough. We say good-bye to Evelyn before she has made any permanent

---

*A popular movie in the thirties.

adjustment to her new life, and at a time when she has just lost her marvelous voice. The novel ends on a note of sadness, against which I protest. Surely the mishaps and setbacks which beset the path of spiritual progress can be recounted with some of the humor which invests one's failures in cookery or falls in learning to ski? Maugham, I believe, would agree with me here. There is nothing gloomy about Larry's career. Unfortunately, however, his creator has gone to the other extreme, and one gets the impression that becoming a saint is just no trouble at all.

And so we come to the last phase of the story, the portrait of the perfected saint. Here, I am sure, I should give up in despair. Nothing short of genius could succeed in such a task. For the mystical experience itself can never be described. It can only be written around, hinted at, dimly reflected in word and deed. So far, the novelists have given us nothing but brilliant glimpses—the incident of the Bishop's candlesticks in *Les Misérables,* the few interviews with Father Zossima, Huxley's sketch of Bruno Rontini. These three men are only minor characters in long and crowded stories. Maugham is greatly to be admired for his more ambitious attempt—even if, as I have indicated above, it is not altogether successful. Tolstoy, toward the end of his career, outlined what might have been a masterpiece. We cannot be sure. The life of *Father Sergius* is told in fewer than fifty pages. Perhaps even Tolstoy felt himself unequal to the undertaking. Perhaps the truly comprehensive religious novel could only be written by a saint—and saints, unfortunately, are not in the habit of writing novels.

THE GITA

The Gita (its full title, *The Bhagavad-Gita,* means *The Blessed Lord's Song*) is often referred to as "the Gospel of Hinduism," because it contains the teachings of Krishna, who may be said to be the Christ of India. (Lest this remark should sound provincial, I hasten to add that Christ, the later comer, might with more justice be called the Krishna of Palestine. There are, indeed, several striking parallel incidents in the recorded lives of these two avatars.) In any case, the Gita is undoubtedly the most frequently read and quoted of the Hindu religious classics. Its teachings were often on the lips of Ramakrishna. It was the daily inspiration of Gandhi. It has influenced the spiritual, cultural, and even the political life of India throughout the centuries, and continues to do so.

The Gita is a most unusual kind of composition, for it has been designed to fit into the middle of another literary work, the Mahabharata. But while the Gita is a religious-philosophical poem, the Mahabharata is an epic—the longest, it is said, in all literature. It consists of about one hundred thousand verses. Its central theme is the story of the descendants of King Bharata (*Maha* means great) and of ancient India, where the Bharatas lived and ruled.

For the purposes of this explanation, it is only necessary to say that Arjuna, the warrior-hero of the story, is about to lead his men in a civil war against the forces of his wicked foster brother Duryodhana, who has tricked him and his own brothers out of their inherited kingdom. The neighbors have been drawn into this quarrel, so that now every chieftain in India has taken sides.

Both sides have appealed to Krishna—who at that time was living on earth in human form—for his help. To both, Krishna has offered the same choice: "Either you can have my kinsmen the Vrishis as your allies in the war, or you can have me alone; but I shall simply be present without taking any part in the fighting." Duryodhana, being a mere opportunist, naturally chooses the physical help of the Vrishnis. Arjuna prefers the moral and spiritual support of his beloved friend Krishna and takes him for his personal charioteer.

Thus far the Mahabharata. Now the Gita takes up the narrative and tells how, just before the battle is to begin, Arjuna asks Krishna to drive him out into the no-man's-land between the two armies. He wants to see the men he is going to fight against. Krishna does as he is asked and Arjuna is shocked— for now he becomes aware that the enemy ranks are filled with his kinsfolk and friends. He does not want to kill these men. He exclaims in desperation that he would rather lose the battle and be killed himself. He will not fight. Krishna, however, rejects this attitude, and a long philosophical dialogue follows—of which more in a moment. The upshot of it is that Arjuna decides that he was wrong. He *will* fight, after all. He has complete confidence in Krishna's judgment. His mind stands firm. His doubts are answered.

At this point, the Gita ends. But here we can turn back to the Mahabharata and continue the story without a break, reading how the battle was then fought on the plain of Kurukshetra and lasted eighteen days, ending with the death of Duryodhana and the complete victory of Arjuna and his brothers. As I said above, the Gita fits perfectly into the Mahabharata narrative; but it was not originally part of it. Most scholars believe that it was composed independently, sometime between the fifth and second centuries B.C.

During the year and a half—approximately from the late summer of 1942 to the beginning of 1944—that I worked with Swami Prabhavananda on the Gita translation, I discussed its philosophy with many different people. However little or much they knew about it, I found that they were almost all agreed on one point: that it sanctioned war. Some found satisfaction in this, others deplored it; but all, I think, were puzzled. Educated in the Christian tradition, they were accustomed to a gospel which is uncompromisingly pacifist. The majority of them set aside the teachings of the gospel, it is true—by the worst of luck, it always seems to happen that this particular war you are fighting is exceptionally necessary and just!—but they were rather shocked when one of their spiritual superiors appeared to be approving the use of military force in general. They themselves, mere humans struggling in the everyday world, might be driven to kill each other; but they wanted Krishna, like Jesus, to stand for a higher ideal.

As a pacifist, I naturally regarded this as a question of major importance. If the Gita really did unconditionally sanction war, then I must reject it as I had long ago rejected the Old Testament. So it was urgently necessary for me to figure out what the Gita *did* mean. What follows is the interpretation which I finally arrived at, under Prabhavananda's guidance. It satisfied my doubts at the time, and it still seems quite valid to me. So I now offer it to any perplexed pacifists who may be among my readers.

First of all, I must say that an objection such as mine was of course not unusual. Gandhi, like many others no doubt, solved it by deciding that the Gita must be regarded as an allegory: Arjuna is the individual soul when it is under the influence of its higher impulses; Krishna is the Atman, the indwelling Godhead; Arjuna's enemies are the soul's evil tendencies, and so forth.

Again, there are those who try to mitigate what they feel to be the Gita's militaristic teaching by pointing out that the conditions under which the battle of Kurukshetra (or any historical battle of that era) was fought were greatly different from those of modern warfare. Kurukshetra was a kind of tournament, governed by all the elaborate and relatively humane rules of classical Indian chivalry. A soldier mounted upon an elephant was not allowed to attack a foot soldier. No man might be struck or shot at while running away. No man might be killed after he had lost his weapons. And the Mahabharata tells us that the opposing armies stopped fighting every day at sunset and even visited each other and fraternized during the night.

This second interpretation of the Gita seems to me irrelevant. Tournament or no tournament, people lost their lives at Kurukshetra in great numbers. And if the Sixth Commandment means anything at all, it means that thou shalt not kill even one single human being, either with a spear or a hydrogen bomb. As for the first interpretation, I must say, despite my most sincere respect for Gandhi, that it does not satisfy me. This question is too serious to be sidestepped in such a manner; and an allegory, however beautiful or ingenious, offers little or no spiritual support in a crisis. If the Gita has any validity, its message must hold good for our own day and age.

To understand the Gita, we must first consider what it is and what it is not. We must consider its setting. When Jesus preached the Sermon on the Mount, he was far from the city and his enemies, in the heart of the countryside. Moreover, he was speaking in general terms, without reference to any immediate crisis or personal problem. It is true that, at a moment of acute danger, in the Garden of Gethsemane, he remained true to his pacifist principles and told Peter to sheathe the sword he had drawn to save his Master from arrest; but it must be remembered that Peter was a dedicated disciple, whom Jesus was training for a missionary life. For him there could be no compromise. He had to be reminded constantly of the highest ideal, that of nonviolence.

In the Gita story, the situation is quite different: Krishna and Arjuna are on a battlefield; Arjuna is a warrior by birth and profession. He belongs to the caste of the Kshatriyas, whose duty it is to be administrators in peacetime and leaders in war. His ideals of conduct are in most respects those of a medieval Christian knight.

Arjuna's problem is an immediate one. He has to make up his mind in this very hour, to fight or not to fight. The problem relates to him *as he is at that moment;* it has nothing to do with any change in his philosophy and ideals which may occur in the future.

The fact that Krishna's teaching in the Gita is inspired by a particular problem of a particular individual at one particular moment is, I believe, a cause of misunderstanding to many readers. We all tend to remember most clearly how a book begins, because we read the opening chapters while our interest is fresh. But the opening chapters deal with Arjuna's case only. Later on, Krishna passes from the particular to the general and teaches the same truths which were afterwards taught by the Buddha and by Jesus. Too late! The superficial reader has got nothing from the Gita but his first impression. Remembering only Arjuna and the battle, he says to himself: Krishna tells us to fight.

Even Arjuna himself questions his motives in shrinking from the battle. After saying, of some of his kinsmen who are among the enemy, "If we kill them, none of us will wish to live," he appeals to Krishna: "Is this real compassion that I feel, or only a delusion? My mind gropes about in darkness. I cannot see where my duty lies."

In answering and teaching Arjuna, Krishna employs two sets of values, relative and absolute. He speaks with two voices. This duality is inherent in his own nature; he is Arjuna's friend and fellow mortal, and he is God. Ramakrishna used to explain that one who knows God is compelled to revert temporarily to a state of ego-consciousness in order to teach others. If the Atman is experienced, then the personality is seen to be a mere mask; the notion that you are "yourself" rather than somebody else becomes meaningless. Seeing God inside means also seeing God outside and everywhere; and how can God teach God? In order to take the measure of Arjuna's ignorance and to answer his doubts, Krishna has to view them from the standpoint of relativity. He must cease for a moment to see Arjuna—and all other men—as a dwelling place of the Atman, and regard him instead as a specific individual whose name is Arjuna, the third son of Pandu and Kunti and the general in command of this army which is about to fight this battle.

But the voice of Krishna's assumed teacher-ego consciousness is often interrupted while another voice speaks through his body; the voice of God. Arjuna does not doubt the genuineness of this voice; he is prepared to believe that Krishna is a divine incarnation. Nevertheless, being only human, he asks for absolute proof; and Krishna supplies this by granting a beautiful but appalling vision of himself as the Lord of the Universe. And now Arjuna realizes just how weak and partial his previous faith had been—necessarily so, perhaps, since man cannot bear conscious companionship with God. He now asks Krishna's pardon:

> Carelessly I called you "Krishna" and "my comrade,"
> Took undying God for friend and fellow-mortal,
> Overbold with love, unconscious of your greatness.

Krishna is quick to reassure Arjuna, by speaking to him again as human to human. Indeed, he tells Arjuna: "You are the friend I chose and love." And Arjuna, reassured, slips back into acceptance of their personal relationship—which is what Krishna evidently wishes. We may infer a similar relationship between Jesus and his disciples after their vision of his transfiguration.

Here are examples of Krishna's two voices:

The Teacher: "Now I will tell you briefly about the nature of him who is called The Deathless by those seers who truly understand the Vedas."

God: "Know only that I exist, and that one atom of myself sustains the universe."

The different in the tone of these two statements makes one gasp. Yet both were uttered by the same mouth and both—such is the inadequacy of language—employ the same word *I*. Throughout the Gita, the teacher-voice and the God-voice of Krishna succeed each other frequently and without warning. No wonder so many readers become confused and explain that their teaching is self-contradictory! We have to keep the distinction clearly in mind when we analyze Krishna's reply to Arjuna's problem.

Krishna begins by dealing with Arjuna's feelings of revulsion, on general grounds. Arjuna shrinks from the act of killing. Krishna reminds him that, in the absolute sense, there is no such act. The Atman, the indwelling Godhead, is the only reality. This body is simply an appearance, the manifestation of a phase of being; its birth, life, and death are alike illusory. In the absolute sense, all talk of killing or being killed is meaningless:

> Some say this Atman
> Is slain, and others
> Call it the slayer:
> They know nothing.
> How can it slay
> Or who shall slay it?

And, in a later passage, speaking as God the creator, sustainer, and dissolver of all things, he says: "All these hosts must die; strike, stay your hand—no matter. Seem to slay. By me these men are slain already."

This is all very well and very true, no doubt. But it is not individually true for Arjuna, because he is not yet in a state of God-consciousness; he still thinks of himself as Arjuna, the warrior. So now Krishna uses his other voice and talks to Arjuna in the language he can best understand, the language of his own moral values:

"Even if you consider this from the standpoint of your own caste duty, you ought not to hesitate; for, to a warrior, there is nothing nobler than a righteous war. . . . But if you refuse to fight this righteous war, you will be turning aside from your duty. You will be a sinner, and disgraced. People will speak ill of you throughout the ages."

For Arjuna, as a member of the warrior caste, the fighting of this battle in defense of his family and property is "righteous." It is his caste duty. In the Gita, we find the caste system presented as a kind of natural order. There are four main castes: the Brahmins, the Kshatriyas, the Vaishyas, and the Sudras—priests, warriors, merchants, and servants. In the last chapter of the Gita, the duties of the four castes are described. Since the four caste types are being considered psychologically rather than sociologically, their names are here translated somewhat differently:

> Seer and leader,
> Provider and server:
> Each has the duty
> Ordained by his nature . . .

> The seer's duty,
> Ordained by his nature,
> Is to be tranquil
> In mind and in spirit
> Self-controlled,
> Austere and stainless,
> Upright, forbearing;
> To follow wisdom,
> To know the Atman,
> Firm of faith
> In the truth that is Brahman.

> The leader's duty,
> Ordained by his nature,
> Is to be bold,
> Unflinching and fearless,
> Subtle of skill
> And open-handed
> Great-hearted in battle,
> A resolute ruler.

Others are born
To the tasks of providing:
These are the traders,
The cultivators,
The breeders of cattle.

To work for all men,
Such is the duty
Ordained for the servers:
This is their nature.

All mankind
Is born for perfection
And each shall attain it,
Will he but follow
His nature's duty.

Much has been said about the evils of the caste system as a social structure; and these criticisms are justified, no doubt, with reference to our own age, into which the mere skeleton has been handed down, bereft of its life breath. But if we think of the castes as psychological categories rather than as social prison cells, we shall be much nearer to understanding what the Gita has to teach about them. It is perfectly obvious that nature makes its own castes: seers, leaders, providers, and servers are to be found among the members of any generation, anywhere on earth. All that the state can do about these basic types is to encourage or discourage the development of some or all of them; but in any case the types will continue to be born.

And whether the state likes it or not, each psychophysical type—and, indeed, each separate individual—has the peculiar ethics and responsibilities which are dictated by its own nature. These constitute what is called in Sanskrit its *dharma,* its "nature's duty." And it is only by following the line of this personal duty that one can grow in spirit. A man must go forward from where he stands. He cannot jump to the Absolute; he must evolve toward it. He cannot arbitrarily assume the duties which belong to another type. If he does so, his whole scale of values will be distorted, his conscience will no longer be able to direct him and he will stray into pride or doubt or mental confusion. "Prefer to die doing your own duty," Krishna tells Arjuna: "The duty of another will bring you into great spiritual danger."

By following his nature's duty, each one of us can attain spiritual perfection; that is Krishna's message. Seven of the saints of southern India were below the lowest caste, Untouchables. Ramakrishna was a Brahmin but he chose disciples from all of the four castes. And likewise among the saints of Christian Europe we find peasants and servants, merchants, soldiers, scholars, doctors, kings, and popes.

Not only is it Arjuna's duty to fight, it is also his *karma*. The Sanskrit word *karma* has a primary and a secondary meaning. A karma is a mental or physical act. It is also the consequences of that act; good, bad, or mixed. Since all Hindu and Buddhist philosophy presupposes a belief in the process of reincarnation, this act may have been performed in some previous life and yet continue to work out its consequences in this one. The law of karma is the natural law by which our present condition is simply the product of our past thoughts and actions, and by which we are always currently engaged in creating our own future.

So Arjuna is no longer a free agent. The act of war is upon him; it has evolved out of his previous actions. He can no longer choose. Krishna reminds him of this: "If, in your vanity, you say 'I will not fight,' your resolve is vain. Your own nature will drive you to the act." At any given moment in time, we are what we are; and our actions express that condition. We cannot run away from our actions because we carry the condition with us. On the highest mountain, in the darkest cave, we must turn at last and accept the consequences of being ourselves. Only through this acceptance can we begin to evolve further. We may choose the battleground. We cannot permanently avoid the battle.

But though the law of karma compels Arjuna to fight—or

refrain from fighting out of mere cowardice, which is morally just as bad—he is still free to make his choice between two ways of performing the action. The right and the wrong performance of action is one of the principal themes of the Gita; Krishna introduces it early in the dialogue, immediately after he has reminded Arjuna of his caste duty. What he now teaches applies not only to Arjuna but to all men at all times in their varying predicaments: "You have the right to work, but for the work's sake only. You have no right to the fruits of work.... Perform every action with your heart fixed on the Supreme Lord. Renounce all attachment to the fruits.... To unite the heart with Brahman and then to act: that is the secret of nonattached work. In the calm of self-surrender, the seers renounce the fruits of their actions, and so reach enlightenment. Then they are free from the bondage of rebirth, and pass to that state which is beyond all evil."

Ramakrishna was fond of saying that you could get the essential message of the Gita by repeating the word several times. "Gita, Gita, Gita," you begin, but then you find yourself saying "ta-Gi, ta-Gi, ta-Gi." *Tagi* means one who has renounced everything for God.

But both Krishna and Ramakrishna made it clear that genuine renunciation is primarily a mental act. For the vast majority of us, it does not involve actually giving up our material possessions and worldly responsibilities. This is where the question has to be asked: what does my dharma demand of me? For the few, there is the vocation to a monastic life; for the many there is the life of the householder. For both, the mental act of renunciation is all-important. If you "renounce" action physically but not mentally, you are simply being lazy. If you break off relationships and give up belongings for the sake of playing the saint or out of a perverse desire for self-torture, you will be filled with bitter secret regret for what you have done, and the renunciation will be false and will bring you no enlightenment.

What, exactly, is meant by mental renunciation? We are told

that we must mentally surrender all our possessions to God, and receive them back from him only on trust, as a workman receives tools from an employer on condition that they are to be used in the employer's service. It may be objected that this kind of renunciation is nothing but a token, a kind of charming poetic fancy. And yet this "fancy" can produce a quality of character which is apparent to the most materialistically minded observer. We have all met men and women who do their jobs with a selfless devotion which sets them apart from the rest of us. We are accustomed to speak of such people as "dedicated," without pausing to ask ourselves in what it is that their dedication consists. If we get to know one of them well, we may even find that his or her dedicated attitude of mind has not been consciously cultivated or willed, or inspired by any religious beliefs; it is, as one says, "natural." And this brings us to the edge of that tremendous mystery we call Personality—a mystery to which the theory of renunciation seems to provide one of the most satisfactory keys.

Nonattachment seems the best translation of the Sanskrit word used in the Gita, yet in our language it has misleading associations. It suggests coldness and indifference and a fatalistic outlook. One can best appreciate its true meaning by considering its opposite. In general, mankind almost always acts with attachment—that is to say, with fear and desire; desire for a certain result and fear that this result will not be obtained. Action produces all kinds of "fruits"—sweet, bitter, or blended in flavor—everything, from a beautiful wife and family, a million dollars and an international reputation, to poverty, disease, and public disgrace. Attachment, therefore, means bondage to any and all of these things. One can be in bondage to failure just as much as to success. Dwelling on mistakes and humiliations is just as egotistical as dwelling on achievements and triumphs.

On the chain of attachment the padlock, so to speak, is egotism. And what is egotism? My obstinate belief that I am

some particular somebody—Mr. Jones, Mademoiselle Du-
pont—rather than the Atman. Get the padlock open and you
have achieved nonattachment. You now know that you are the
Atman and that every action is done for the sake of the Atman
alone. Work has become sacramental. No fruits of it are desired,
no consequences are feared. The work is its own reward; and
as long as it is done to the very best of one's ability, that reward
can never be withheld. There are, of course, many degrees of
nonattachment; it grows by practice, and as it grows and the
sense of the Atman's presence increases, the need for further
action will gradually fall away from us. The law of karma will
cease to operate, and we shall be set free from the cycle of birth,
death, and rebirth.

It follows therefore, theoretically at least, that *every* action—
under certain circumstances and for certain individuals—may
be a stepping-stone to spiritual growth, *if* it is done in the spirit
of nonattachment. This is a shocking thought, but we must
accept it in principle if we are to accept the Gita's teaching. All
good and evil is relative to the individual point of growth. For
each individual, certain acts are absolutely wrong. Probably
there are acts which are absolutely wrong or absolutely right for
every individual alive on earth today. But, from the highest
viewpoint, there can be neither good nor evil.

> The Lord is everywhere
> And always perfect;
> What does he care for man's sin
> Or the righteousness of man?

Because Krishna is speaking as God, he can take this attitude, and advise Arjuna to fight. Because Arjuna has reached
this particular stage in his development, he can kill his enemies
and actually be doing his duty.

There is no question, here, of doing evil that good may
come. The Gita does not countenance this kind of opportunism.
Arjuna is to do the best he knows at this moment, in order that

he may later pass beyond that best to better. Later, through the practice of nonattachment, his responsibilities as a leader and warrior will fall away from him; and when that happens it will have become wrong for him to fight or to do any act of violence. Doing the evil you know to be evil will never bring good. It will lead only to more evil, more attachment, more ignorance.

So the Gita neither sanctions war nor condemns it. Regarding no action as of absolute universal value, for good or for evil, it cannot possibly do either. Its teaching should warn us not to dare to judge others. And how can we ever prescribe our neighbor's duty when it is so hard for us to know our own? After much self-analysis, you may decide that your own scruples are genuine and that you can wholeheartedly take your stand as a pacifist—though the decision is certainly difficult enough, with no Krishna to tell you your duty. But the pacifist must respect Arjuna, just as Arjuna must respect the pacifist. Both are going toward the same goal, if they are really sincere. There is an underlying solidarity between them, if each one follows without compromise the path upon which he finds himself. For we can only help others to do their nature's duty by doing what we ourselves believe to be right. It is the one truly disinterested social act.

On Translating the Gita

Our work on the Gita was, for me, not only a literary problem but an education in Vedanta philosophy. Even if the result had not been intended for publication, I should have felt that every moment of it was worthwhile. For the slow thorough-going process of translating a text—considering all the significance of each word and often spending a day on three or four verses—is the ideal way to study, *if* you have a teacher like Prabhavananda.

The swami's English was fluent and his knowledge of Sanskrit equally good. As regards the latter, he had an advantage in being a Bengali—for the Bengali language has about the same relation to Sanskrit as modern Greek has to classical Greek. Sanskrit is no longer spoken, except when monks, priests, or scholars from different parts of India use it as their only common language, just as an Irish Catholic priest might talk to a German priest in Latin. At that time, I knew no Sanskrit whatsoever; even today I have absolutely no knowledge of its grammar and could easily write down my little vocabulary on one side of a postcard. My share in the collaboration was therefore secondary. Prabhavananda told me the meaning of a phrase; we then considered how this meaning could best be conveyed in English.

The problem was more difficult than it sounds, because the Gita itself is a much more complex work than it at first appears to be. Although it is relatively short, it is not a uniform whole— either from a philosophical or a literary standpoint. Indeed, it is as various as the Bible. There is no need to prove this point by claiming, as some scholars have done, that certain portions of it may have been added later; that is a vexed question and anyhow immaterial. That the existing version of the Gita has at least four distinct aspects, any careful reader can see for himself.

Unlike the Bible, the Gita is all in verse, but this is not to say that it is all good poetry. Some of the material is essentially poetic, but other parts of it have merely been forced into verse form, no doubt in order to make them easier to memorize. In India today, there are still many people who can recite the whole Gita by heart. It is often chanted or read in its entirety at important religious festivals.

The Gita can be said to be partly an epic, partly a prophetic vision, partly a gospel, partly a philosophical exposition.

As I have already said, it is constructed to fit into an epic poem; its opening chapter continues in the mood of the Mahabharata, with a background of menacing war trumpets. The narrative style is still that of the classical epic:

"Then Krishna, subduer of the senses, thus requested by Arjuna, the conqueror of sloth, drove that most splendid of chariots into a place between the two armies, confronting Bhisma, Drona and all those other rulers of the earth. And he said: 'O Prince, behold the assembled Kurus!' "

Yet in the very next chapter, Krishna talks like this: "I have explained to you the true nature of the Atman. Now listen to the method of Karma Yoga. . . . " This is certainly not the tone of an epic character; it is a teacher of philosophy addressing his pupil.

Then again, in the eleventh chapter, we have poetry in the prophetic manner; something akin to the visions of Isaiah and the book of Revelation. Krishna is transfigured and appears to Arjuna in his true nature, as Lord of the Universe: " . . . speaking from unnumerable mouths, seeing with a myriad eyes, of many marvelous aspects, adorned with countless divine ornaments, brandishing all kinds of heavenly weapons, wearing celestial garlands and the raiment of paradise, anointed with perfumes of heavenly fragrance, full of revelations, resplendent, boundless, of ubiquitous regard. Suppose a thousand suns should rise together into the sky: such is the glory of the Shape of Infinite God."

And lastly, scattered throughout the book, we find passages of dialogue which seem almost dateless in their simplicity, belonging to no particular epoch. As in the Christian Gospel, man and incarnate God speak together as friend to friend:

Arjuna: "When a man goes astray from the path to Brahman, he has missed both lives, the worldly and the spiritual. He has no support anywhere. Is he not lost, as a broken cloud is lost in the sky?"

Krishna: "No, my son. That man is not lost, either in this world or the next. No one who seeks Brahman ever comes to an evil end."

How is the translator to render these different aspects of the Gita and reconcile them with each other? It is clear that no single uniform style will be adequate. Basic English cannot deal with the ornateness of the poetic passages; poetic language cannot convey the precise meanings of the philosophical terms; academic language is too awkward for the directness of the colloquial passages. And besides, Sanskrit differs radically from modern English. The Gita is phrased with the terseness of a telegram. It is full of technical philosophic words for which we have often no direct equivalent. And it is based upon a very definite conception of the universe which is implicit in its statements and must be explained to the modern reader. Here are some of the key words in the Gita's vocabulary. Each one is a problem for the translator.

Brahman is the Reality in its universal aspect, as opposed to the *Atman* which is the Reality within ourselves. The Reality is always the Reality, one and undivided; these two words merely designate two viewpoints from which it can be considered. Look inward and you see the Atman, look outward and you see Brahman; but Atman and Brahman are really one. . . . Very well, now how are you going to translate? If you call Brahman "God," you are apt to create a misunderstanding—at least in the mind of any Christian or Jew. For "God" is naturally associated by them with the Jehovah of the Old Testament, and Jehovah is God-with-attributes; he is alternately stern and merciful, he wills certain events, he favors the children of Israel. There is a word in Sanskrit for God-with-attributes; it is *Ishwara*. But Brahman is the Reality without attributes, without will, without moods. It is Brahman seen within maya, that appears as Ishwara. If you translate Brahman as "The Reality" or "The Absolute," you still have to explain what you mean; these overworked words have become so imprecise. If you use "The Godhead," as has been done in translations from Meister Eckhart, you seem nearer to a definition, since the dictionary says it means "the essential being of God." But somehow this starkly medieval word sounds odd and unfitting on the lips of Krishna.

The Atman, it has been said, is the Reality within ourselves. But when one searches for a single English word to say this, it cannot be found, because Christianity does not quite accept this concept. "Soul" is out of the question; the soul is not God. "Spirit" is utterly vague. Many translators call the Atman "The Self"; but this word has unfortunate associations with "selfishness." Moreover, there are certain passages in which the translator is then forced to speak of the Self with a big *S* meaning the Atman and the self with a small *s* meaning the personal ego; a distinction which is lost when the words are read aloud. And an occasionally unavoidable use of the possessive form produces the horrible combination "his Self." You can more or less adequately describe the Atman as "God Immanent" and Brahman as "God Transcendent," but these phrases are too awkward for frequent repetition and they have the dryness of Victorian theology.

The meanings of the word *karma* have already been discussed. Here, the translator cannot hope to find absolute equivalents. Even in its primary meaning, karma cannot always be translated by the same word; one has to alternate between "action" and "work" according to the context. As for the secondary meaning of karma, what is the use of translating it as "the effect of a deed"? The expression is falsely simple: further explanation is absolutely necessary. And the law of karma—well, how is any Western reader to know what that is, until he has been told in at least one fairly long sentence?

Explanation at length is also unavoidable in dealing with the very important words *prakriti* and *maya*. It has been said that Brahman is without attributes. What, then, is the relation of Brahman to the universe? Brahman cannot be said to create, preserve, or destroy. It is the power or effect of Brahman— other than Brahman yet inseparable from Brahman, just as heat is inseparable from fire—which forms the stuff of all mind and matter. This power of Brahman is called prakriti. Since prakriti is by definition coexistent with Brahman, the universe must also be thought of as being without beginning or end—though it may pass through phases of potentiality and expression, during which it seems to be alternately created and destroyed. Each of us has, so to speak, one foot in the absolute and one in the relative; our nature is the Atman, our substance is prakriti. Enlightenment is the recognition of a situation which already exists, namely that we are the Atman essentially and prakriti only relatively. Nevertheless, prakriti cannot be said to be unreal. Brahman lends it a relative reality. This universe and Ishwara its master are related to Brahman inseparably. The many aspects of Ishwara, God-within-the-universe, are projected by the one Brahman.

And so we must come to maya—almost the only Sanskrit word which many people know, or believe they know. They believe it means "illusion," and they are wrong. Actually, the words *maya* and *prakriti* are interchangeable. They do not *mean* illusion, but from the absolute viewpoint they *are* illusion; since, when Brahman is known, prakriti is seen to have only a relative existence. Some translators—the kind who are determined to translate at any cost—have rendered prakriti as "nature" or "primordial matter." This is the best way to confirm a lazy reader in his laziness. "Ah yes—nature," he murmurs to himself and passes on, without having made the least effort to understand what the term is being used to mean.

Finally, there are the three *gunas: sattwa, rajas,* and *tamas.* Modern science tells us that matter is energy. The cosmology of Vedanta also contains this concept. Prakriti is said to be composed of three gunas, or forces. During a phase of potentiality—when the universe has been apparently destroyed and is actually in a "seed-state"—these gunas are in perfect equilibrium, and prakriti is just undifferentiated "matter-stuff." What we call creation is the upsetting of this equilibrium. The gunas forthwith begin to enter into an ever increasing variety of combinations which are the various forms of mind and matter that make up the universe during its phases of expression. The universe continues to develop in this manner until it can, as it were, no longer bear the burden of its own complexity; at this point it dissolves, returning to its potential phase, and thus to ultimate rebirth. Such is the unending cyclic process.

Each of the three gunas has a character, and it is the exact proportion to which each of the three is present in any given object that determines the nature of that object. One guna is of course always predominant over the others, in order that disequilibrium may be maintained; since without disequilibrium there can be no expression.

In the physical sphere, sattwa embodies all that is pure and fine, rajas embodies violence and movement, tamas the quality of solidity and resistance. Sattwa, for example, predominates in sunlight, rajas in an erupting volcano, tamas in a block of granite. In the psychological sphere, sattwa expresses itself as tranquility, purity, calmness; rajas as passion, restlessness, aggressive activity; tamas as stupidity, laziness, inertia. The gunas also represent the three stages in the evolution of any particular entity. Sattwa is the essence of the form to be realized; tamas is the inherent obstacle to that realization; rajas is the power by which that obstacle is removed and the essential form made manifest. For example, a sculptor gets an idea (sattwa) for a figure of a horse. To make the idea manifest, he needs granite (tamas) and muscular power (rajas). He feels lazy (tamas) but overcomes the laziness by his determination (rajas), and so, in due course, this idea of the horse (sattwa) is given physical expression. From this it is clear that all three gunas are absolutely necessary for any act of creation. Sattwa alone would be just an unrealized idea, rajas without sattwa would be mere undirected energy, rajas without tamas would be like a lever without a fulcrum.

I have taken three paragraphs to explain what the gunas are—yet there are many translators who offer one-word English equivalents. Here are five different ones, taken from five versions of the Gita: The qualities, the moods, the elements, the strands, the dispositions. And for the individual gunas there is an equal variety of renderings. Sattwa is translated as purity, goodness, truth; rajas as fieriness, passion, greed; tamas as ignorance, dullness, gloom. Not one of these is absolutely wrong; not one is right in all possible contexts, physical and psychological. What, for example, is the uninitiated reader to understand by the goodness of X rays, the greed of a volcano or the gloom of a table? And if we use different words to suit different contexts, we can no longer pretend to have an exact terminology with which to express the Gita's teaching.

There is, of course, an alternative: to decide that certain much-used terms must remain in the original Sanskrit and be explained in footnotes or an appendix. This is probably the lesser evil. But the translator must keep the Sanskrit down to a minimum. There are all too many versions which contain verses like this:

"Those who know Me with the *Adhibhuta,* the *Adhidaiva,* and the *Adhiyajna,* continue to know me even at the time of death, steadfast in mind."

Then, again, there is the snare of literalness. I have already remarked that Sanskrit differs greatly in its construction from English. A certain degree of paraphrase would seem to be absolutely necessary, but a very subtle line divides paraphrase from comment and exposition. The translator must decide just how far he can go. If he does not go far enough, he will produce something like the last radio message from a sinking ship: "By the intellect set in patience; mind placed in the Self; making by degrees should attain quietude; not even anything should think."

SELECTIONS FROM THE GITA

Editor's Note

The following is a selection from *The Bhagavad-Gita: The Song of God,* translated by Swami Prabhavananda and Christopher Isherwood. Since the story line has been described elsewhere in this volume, the verses have been selected solely on the basis of their beauty and meaning.

It is interesting to note how this translation came about:

Swami Prabhavananda and Christopher Isherwood were in Palm Springs for a brief vacation. The swami didn't care for the current translations of the Gita. None of them seemed to convey the beauty or deep spirit of the original Sanskrit. He asked Isherwood if he would help him with a new translation, and of course Isherwood agreed.

Swami Prabhavananda remembers: "I translated and Chris edited. A friend of ours, Peggy Kiskadden, came and read what we had done but could not understand it. Then we went to Aldous Huxley. Chris read our version aloud and Aldous listened.

"Aldous said, 'No, that's not right yet. Forget that Krishna is speaking to the Hindus in Sanskrit. Forget that this is a translation. Think that Krishna is speaking to an American audience in English.'

"Aldous then told Chris which style to use for verse and Chris rewrote the whole eleventh chapter of the Gita in the style of Tennyson, I believe. We all liked what he had done. After a week, the book was finished. Chris was inspired."

Do not say:
"God gave us this delusion."
You dream you are the doer,
You dream that action is done,
You dream that action bears fruit.
It is your ignorance,
It is the world's delusion
That gives you these dreams.

The Lord is everywhere
And always perfect:
What does He care for man's sin
Or the righteousness of man?

The Atman is the light:
The light is covered by darkness:
This darkness is delusion:
That is why we dream.

When the light of the Atman
Drives out our darkness
That light shines forth from us,
A sun in splendor,
The revealed Brahman.

The devoted dwell with Him,
They know Him always
There in the heart,
Where action is not.
He is all their aim.
Made free by His Knowledge
From past uncleanness
Of deed or of thought,
They find the place of freedom,
The place of no return.*

---

*The state in which one is no longer subject to rebirth, because illumination has been attained.

When senses touch objects
The pleasures therefrom
Are like wombs that bear sorrow.
They begin, they are ended:
They bring no delight to the wise.

Already, here on earth,
Before his departure,
Let man be the master
Of every impulse
Lust-begotten
Or fathered by anger:
Thus he finds Brahman,
Thus he is happy.

Only that yogi
Whose joy is inward,
Inward his peace,
And his vision inward
Shall come to Brahman
And know Nirvana.*

---

*The state of union with Brahman.

Let him who would climb
In meditation
To heights of the highest
Union with Brahman
Take for his path
The yoga of action:
Then when he nears
That height of oneness
His acts will fall from him,
His path will be tranquil.

Who knows the Atman
Knows that happiness
Born of pure knowledge:
The joy of sattwa.
Deep his delight
After strict self-schooling:
Sour toil at first
But at last what sweetness,
The end of sorrow.

Senses also
Have joy in their marriage
With things of the senses,
Sweet at first
But at last how bitter:
Steeped in rajas,
That pleasure is poison.

Bred of tamas
Is brutish contentment
In stupor and sloth
And obstinate error:
Its end, its beginning
Alike are delusion.

Worn-out garments
Are shed by the body:
Worn-out bodies
Are shed by the dweller
Within the body.
New bodies are donned
By the dweller, like garments.

Not wounded by weapons,
Not burned by fire,
Not dried by the wind,
Not wetted by water:
Such is the Atman,

Not dried, not wetted,
Not burned, not wounded,
Innermost element,
Everywhere, always,
Being of beings,
Changeless, eternal,
For ever and ever.

This Atman cannot be manifested to the senses, or thought about by the mind. It is not subject to modification. Since you know this, you should not grieve.

When a man can still the senses
I call him illumined.
The recollected mind is awake
In the knowledge of the Atman
Which is dark night to the ignorant:
The ignorant are awake in their sense-life
Which they think is daylight:
To the seer it is darkness.

Water flows continually into the ocean
But the ocean is never disturbed:
Desire flows into the mind of the seer
But he is never disturbed.
The seer knows peace:
The man who stirs up his own lusts
Can never know peace.
He knows peace who has forgotten desire.
He lives without craving:
Free from ego, free from pride.

This is the state of enlightenment in Brahman:
A man does not fall back from it
Into delusion.
Even at the moment of death
He is alive in that enlightenment:
Brahman and he are one.

The abstinent run away from what they desire
But carry their desires with them:
When a man enters Reality,
He leaves his desires behind him.

Even a mind that knows the path
Can be dragged from the path:
The senses are so unruly.
But he controls the senses
And recollects the mind
And fixes it on me.
I call him illumined.

Thinking about sense-objects
Will attach you to sense-objects;
Grow attached, and you become addicted;
Thwart your addiction, it turns to anger;

Be angry, and you confuse your mind;
Confuse your mind, you forget the lesson of experience;
Forget experience, you lose discrimination;
Lose discrimination, and you miss life's only purpose.

When he has no lust, no hatred,
A man walks safely among the things of lust and hatred.
To obey the Atman
Is his peaceful joy:
Sorrow melts
Into that clear peace:
His quiet mind
Is soon established in peace.

The uncontrolled mind
Does not guess that the Atman is present:
How can it meditate?
Without medication, where is peace?
Without peace, where is happiness?

The wind turns a ship
From its course upon the waters:
The wandering winds of the senses
Cast man's mind adrift
And turn his better judgment from its course.

When goodness grows weak,
When evil increases,
I make myself a body.

In every age I come back
To deliver the holy,
To destroy the sin of the sinner,
To establish righteousness.

He who knows the nature
Of my task and my holy birth
Is not reborn
When he leaves this body:
He comes to me.

Flying from fear,
From lust and anger,
He hides in me
His refuge, his safety:
Burnt clean in the blaze of my being,
In me many find home.

Whatever wish men bring me in worship,
That wish I grant them.
Whatever path men travel
Is my path:
No matter where they walk
It leads to me.

ARJUNA:

Restless man's mind is,
So strongly shaken
In the grip of the senses:
Gross and grown hard
With stubborn desire
For what is worldly.
How shall he tame it?
Truly, I think
The wind is no wilder.

SRI KRISHNA:

Yes, Arjuna, the mind is restless, no doubt, and hard to subdue. But
it can be brought under control by constant practice, and by the
exercise of dispassion. Certainly, if a man has no control over his ego,
he will find this yoga difficult to master. But a self-controlled man can
master it, if he struggles hard, and uses the right means.

ARJUNA:

Suppose a man has faith, but does not struggle hard enough? His
mind wanders away from the practice of yoga and he fails to reach
perfection. What will become of him then?

When a man goes astray from the path to Brahman, he has missed
both lives, the worldly and the spiritual. He has no support anywhere.
Is he not lost, as a broken cloud is lost in the sky?

This is the doubt that troubles me, Krishna; and only you can
altogether remove it from my mind. Let me hear your answer.

SRI KRISHNA:

No, my son. That man is not lost, either in this world or the next. No
one who seeks Brahman ever comes to an evil end.

Even if a man falls away from the practice of yoga, he will still win
the heaven of the doers of good deeds, and dwell there many long
years. After that, he will be reborn into the home of pure and prosperous
parents. He may even be born into a family of illumined yogis. But
such a birth in this world is more difficult to obtain.

He will then regain that spiritual discernment which he acquired in his former body; and so he will strive harder than ever for perfection. Because of his practices in the previous life, he will be driven on toward union with Brahman, even in spite of himself. For the man who has once asked the way to Brahman goes further than any mere fulfiller of the Vedic rituals.

PART V

THE WISHING TREE

THE WISHING TREE

One afternoon, when the children are tired of running around the garden and have gathered for a moment on the lawn, their uncle tells them the story of the Kalpataru tree.

The Kalpataru, he explains, is a magic tree. If you speak to it and tell it a wish, or if you lie down under it and think or even dream a wish, then that wish will be granted. The children are half skeptical, half impressed. Truly—it'll give you anything you ask for? *Anything?* Yes, the uncle assures them solemnly: anything in the world. The audience grins and whistles with amazement. Then someone wants to know: what does it look like?

The uncle, pleased at the success of his storytelling, casts his eye around the garden and points, almost at random: "That's one of them, over there."

But this is too much of a good thing. The children are mistrustful now. They look quickly around at their uncle's face and see in it that all-too-familiar expression which children learn to detect in the faces of grown-ups. "He's just fooling us!" they exclaim, indignantly. And they scatter again to their play.

However, children do not forget so easily. Each single one of them, down to the youngest, has privately resolved to talk to the Kalpataru tree at the first opportunity. They have been trained by their parents to believe in wishing. They wish when they see the new moon; or when they get the wishbone of a chicken. They wish at Christmas and just before their birthdays. They know, by experience, that some of these wishes come true. Maybe the tree is a magic tree, maybe it isn't—but, anyhow, what can you lose?

The tree which the uncle pointed out to his nephews and nieces is tall and beautiful, with big feathery branches like the wings of huge birds. It looks somehow queer and exotic among the sturdy familiar trees of that northern climate. There is a vague family tradition that it was planted years ago by a grandfather who had traveled in the Orient. What nobody, including the uncle, suspects is that this tree really *is* a Kalpataru tree— one of the very few in the whole country.

The Kalpataru listens attentively to the children's wishes— its leaves can catch even the faintest whisper—and, in due time, it grants them all. Most of the wishes are very unwise—many of them end in indigestion or tears—but the wishing tree fulfills them, just the same: it is not interested in giving good advice.

Years pass. The children are all men and women now. They have long since forgotten the Kalpataru tree and the wishes they told it—indeed, it is part of the tree's magic to make them forget. Only—and this is the terrible thing about the Kalpataru magic—the gifts which it gave the children were not really gifts, but only like the links of a chain—each wish was linked to another wish, and so on, and on. The older the children grow, the more they wish; it seems as if they could never wish enough. At first, the aim of their lives was to get their wishes granted; but, later on, it is just the opposite—their whole effort is to find wishes which will be very hard, or even impossible, to fulfill. Of course, the Kalpataru tree can grant any wish in the world—but they have forgotten it, and the garden where it stands. All that remains is the fever it has kindled in them by the granting of that first, childish wish.

You might suppose that these unlucky children, as they became adults, would be regarded as lunatics, with horror or pity, by their fellow human beings. But more people have, in their childhood, wished at the Kalpataru tree than is generally supposed. The kind of madness from which the children are suffering is so common that nearly everybody has a streak of it in his or her nature—so it is regarded as perfectly right and proper. "You want to watch those kids," older people say of them, approvingly: "They've got plenty of ambition. Yes, sir— they're going places." And these elders, in their friendly desire to see this ambition rewarded, are always suggesting to the children new things to wish for. The children listen to them attentively and respectfully, believing that here must be the best guides to the right conduct of one's life.

Thanks to these helpful elders, they know exactly what are the things one must wish for in this world. They no longer have to ask themselves such childish questions as: "Do I honestly want this?" "Do I really desire that?" For the wisdom of past generations has forever decided what is, and what is not, desirable and enjoyable and worthwhile. Just obey the rules of the world's wishing game and you need never bother about your feelings. As long as you wish for the right things, you may be quite sure you really want them, no matter what disturbing doubts may trouble you from time to time. Above all, you must wish continually for money and power—more and more money, and more and more power—because, without these two basic wishes, the whole game of wishing becomes impossible—not only for yourself, but for others as well. By not wishing, you are actually spoiling their game—and that, everybody agrees, is not merely selfish, but dangerous and criminal, too.

And so the men and women who were shown the Kalpataru tree in the garden of their childhood, grow old and sick and come near to their end. Then, perhaps, at last, very dimly, they begin to remember something about the Kalpataru and the garden, and how all this madness of wishing began. But this remembering is very confused. The furthest that most of them go is to say to themselves: "Perhaps I ought to have asked it for something different." Then they rack their poor old brains to think what that wish, which would have solved every problem and satisfied every innermost need, could possibly have been. And there are many who imagine they have found the answer when they exclaim: "All my other wishes were mistaken. Now I wish the wish to end all wishes. I wish for death."

But, in that garden, long ago, there was one child whose experience was different from that of all the others. For, when he had crept out of the house at night, and stood alone, looking up into the branches of the tree, the real nature of the Kalpataru was suddenly revealed to him. For him, the Kalpataru was not the pretty magic tree of his uncle's story—it did not exist to grant the stupid wishes of children—it was unspeakably terrible and grand. It was his father and his mother. Its roots held the world together, and its branches reached behind the stars. Before the beginning, it had been—and it would be, always.

Wherever that child went, as a boy, as a youth, and as a man, he never forgot the Kalpataru tree. He carried the secret knowledge of it in his heart. He was wise in its wisdom and strong in its strength; its magic never harmed him. Nobody ever heard him say, "I wish," or "I want"—and, for this reason, he was not very highly thought of in the world. As for his brothers and sisters, they sometimes referred to him, rather apologetically, as "a bit of a saint," by which they meant that he was a trifle crazy.

But the boy himself did not feel that he had to apologize or explain anything. He knew the secret of the Kalpataru, and that was all he needed to know. For, even as an old man, his heart was still the heart of that little child who stood breathless in the moonlight beneath the great tree and thrilled with such wonder and awe and love that he utterly forgot to speak his wish.

DATES OF PUBLICATION

Unless otherwise noted below, all of the essays in *The Wishing Tree* were first published in *Vedanta and the West*. The dates of publication are listed below.

"How I Came to Vedanta," from *An Approach to Vedanta* (Hollywood: Vedanta Press, 1963).

"What Is Vedanta?" (November/December 1944).

"What Vedanta Means to Me" (September/October, 1951).

"Vedanta and the West" (May/June 1951).

"Hypothesis and Belief" (May/June 1944).

"On the Love of God," published as a preface to Swami Prabhavananda's *Narada's Way of Divine Love* (Hollywood: Vedanta Press, 1971).

"Religion Without Prayers" (July/August 1946).

"Who Is Ramakrishna?" (July/August 1957).

"The Home of Ramakrishna" (July/August 1958).

"On Swami Vivekananda" (November/December 1962).

"On the Writings of Swami Vivekananda," published as a foreword to *Meditation and Its Methods* (Hollywood: Vedanta Press, 1974).

"Vivekananda and Sarah Bernhardt" (July/August 1943).

"Swami Shivananda: A Man of God" (January/February 1950).

"On Girish Ghosh," an unpublished lecture delivered in Santa Barbara, California, circa 1957.

"The Writer and Vedanta" (March/April 1961).

"The Problem of the Religious Novel" (March/April 1946).

"The Gita," from *An Approach to Vedanta* (Hollywood: Vedanta Press, 1963).

"Selections from the Gita," excepts from *The Bhagavad-Gita: The Song of God,* trans. Swami Prabhavananda and Christopher Isherwood (Hollywood: Vedanta Press, 1944).

"The Wishing Tree" (November/December 1943).